FACE-TO-FACE WITH THE BEAST

Crespi stood, looked back—and saw several glistening black shapes, no less frightening in the daylight, creeping out of the rip in the stone. They were coming.

Crespi took a few steps and then fell, got up and kept going in spite of the terrible pain; hell was behind him.

A bolt of agonizing pain in his side as a giant, dark claw grasped his broken ribs. He was spun around, vaguely aware that he screamed but unable to hear the depths of terror in his own voice when he saw the thing that held him.

A giant, seething animal, crowned with a massive, gleaming comb of black. She had two pairs of arms, the ones that held him long and articulated, the talons sharp and piercing. Blood ran from the wounds in his chest, and he saw behind her another entrance to the hellish cavern—her lair. For this monstrosity was surely the queen, half again as tall as her drone minions, hissing and screaming at him with no sound—

She brought him closer, close enough to see the pearly spittle across her steel teeth. The horrible jaws opened, impossibly wide, and he saw the second set extend, slowly, so slowly—

Crespi struggled, screamed, his dusty boots kicking against her skull, but she was too strong, carried him to her dripping jaws with ease. He was going to die.

I'm sorry, sorry . . . .

Don't miss any of these exciting *Aliens*, *Aliens vs. Predator* and *Predator* adventures from Bantam Books!

Be sure to look for all of Bantam's classic Star Trek *novels:*

Complete your Bantam Star Wars *library:*

ALIENS™

LABYRINTH

S. D. Perry

*Based on the Twentieth Century Fox motion
pictures, the designs of H. R. Giger,
and the Dark Horse graphic novel
ALIENS: LABYRINTH
by Jim Woodring and Kilian Plunkett*

BANTAM BOOKS
New York • Toronto • London • Sydney • Auckland

ALIENS: LABYRINTH

A Bantam Spectra Book / April 1996
SPECTRA and the portrayal of a boxed "s" are trademarks of
Bantam Books, a division of Bantam Doubleday Dell Publishing
Group, Inc.

ISBN 0-553-57491-4

Published simultaneously in the United States and Canada

Bantam Books are published by Bantam Books, a division of
Bantam Doubleday Dell Publishing Group, Inc. Its trademark,
consisting of the words "Bantam Books" and the portrayal of a
rooster, is Registered in U.S. Patent and Trademark Office and
in other countries. Marca Registrada. Bantam Books, 1540
Broadway, New York, New York 10036.

PRINTED IN THE UNITED STATES OF AMERICA

RAD   10 9 8 7 6 5 4 3 2 1

To my talented and creative Dad, for the work, and the introduction to a career that lets me sleep late; and to Mÿk, the man who's gonna marry me—you're loopy as a goose, dearheart, and I can't wait.

FACE

NECK

IMMUNIZATION
PAPERS
PAUL

I fled Him, down the nights and down the days; I fled Him, down the arches of the years; I fled Him, down the labyrinthine ways of my own mind; and in the mist of tears I hid from Him, and under running laughter.

—Francis Thompson, 1893

Prologue

There was a darkness gathered, a dull measure of black even in the murky half-light that shadowed the nest. Movement, measured and animal, there in the unclean chamber. An unfolding of form, a sound like bone against bone—and then the low, feral hiss . . . inhuman. Alien.

The others, the lucky ones—they were surely dead. Or beyond knowing what life was, it was the same; insanity had smiled down at them, lent its fevered, mindless touch to the last vestiges of their souls. His family, his friends. He had heard, felt it deep inside, had known it as his heart died and his reason cried for release, echoing the distant, demented screams of his loved ones.

The midnight creature moved closer, followed by another. He felt a glimmer of something like hope, a delicate glow in his mind's eye. Could it be death, then? Were there miracles in hell?

There was nothing left to fight for, no reason to try. The demons reached out for him, hard and black, and he offered no resistance, nothing but a twitch at the corners of his mouth, a strange lifting that came unbidden and unanticipated—

A grin. When all of your senses have been brutally raped in the dark, all you've cherished taken away . . . death was redundant.

And he was so startled by the revelation that he started to laugh, not even hearing the hoarse and awful croaks that spilled from his shredded throat and reverberated down through the labyrinth of his pain.

1

For a time there was nothing, the blankness of absolute space with no stars, no movement. Void. And then at the end of eternity, a single pinpoint of flashing green, sudden and beautiful in the darkness, a chime of motion and light, a birdsong—followed closely by a bitter, sticky taste like ancient sour sweat.

Crespi raised his eyebrows and then slowly blinked, squinting at the dim lights overhead. The pulse of green reappeared, a blinking cursor on the comp screen at his feet, joined by a distinctly annoying chirp. Much uglier in reality. His eyelids drifted down, back to the sweet abyss—

Beep!

"Yeah, yeah," he muttered, and sat up slowly. Felt that unfocused hatred for being forced awake. He glared blearily at a spot on the floor for a time, fully aware of every ache in every muscle; he itched but didn't have the energy to scratch and his mouth tasted like an old boot. Almost a year older, and he felt every minute of it.

The few . . . the proud . . . the fatigued . . .

The comp bleated again and Crespi scowled in its direction, then peered closer at the focusing words.

//Wake up, Tony, I'm six months older than you were. O Death, where is Thy stinger? Ouch! *2467He*//

Crespi smiled in spite of himself. Heller. "Uh huh. Not funny, honey." He yawned widely and reached for the code slates racked up beneath the screen, then tapped at transmit.

His voice was uneven, his throat dry, but he did his best to sound official. Heller was a wit, good for morale, but tended to be a bit too casual with his superiors. On the other hand, he *was* a pilot; seemed to be some kind of requisite . . .

"This is Colonel Doctor Crespi. How are we?" He raised his arms over his head and stretched, yawning again.

"This is Lieutenant Colonel Heller. We're fine, sir. *Arkham* is due to dock with *Innominata* at 0900—" There was a pause, and Crespi could hear the grin in the pilot's voice. "How did you sleep, sir?"

Crespi scruffed at his stubbled cheeks. "Like plastic. Anything to release?"

"Yes, *sir*. Coming through now."

Crespi shook his head and nocked his slate into the comp's drive as the screen flickered up codes. Eyes only.

"Thank you, uh, Lieutenant Colonel. I'll see you on the bridge in twenty."

"Sir."

Heller went out in a screech of static that probably wasn't accidental. Crespi rapped at the discom, frowning. Eyes only? *That'd* give the crew something to chew on, as if there wasn't enough already.

He sat on the edge of his sleep chamber and printed the screen, grimacing at the low ache in his abdominal muscles. Not enough time to work out, not if he wanted a shower . . .

The message glowed to life and Crespi forgot about exercise for the moment. Coded NPII7, top priority.

//Tony—CVL says SEO NNJB907H gives you full discretion. You are authorized to assume at will /by force if necessary/ emergency command of *Innominata* for probable cause by NNJB907H.//

Cited and verified, holy hell, and straight from the horse's ass—Admiral D. U. Pickman, head of ETops. The man was a fanatic for the drone plague, had personally been responsible for at least a hundred covert wipes—including the Waller disaster on Myna 8. Fifty civilians and over a dozen Marines dead, even the spindocs had been fucked on that one.

Probable cause? The admiral screamed "nest" at every shadow, so that was unlikely—but if even half of what he'd heard about *Innominata* was true . . .

"Good *morning*," he rasped, and went to take a shower.

Eighteen minutes later Crespi tabbed his boots and then stood for inspection. The face in the mirror looked haggard, old, in spite of the shave and shower. He was in good (hell, *very* good) shape for forty-one TS, but the lines on his face told their own tales.

He sighed and reached for his cap, wondering vaguely why he wasn't more excited. The chance to work with Paul Church, even as an assistant, was an honor; Doctor Church had broken ground some ten years back with a series of biological tests on a space-borne virus that had wiped out three colonies of terraformers on two different worlds. Church had discovered it, classified it, and formulated a serum while the Earth's top scientists were still unpacking their test tubes.

There had been times in his grunt days when the dream of doing such prestigious research was all that had kept him going, and he had worked hard to get here, he had *earned* it.

And yet he felt like shit. The aftermath of the deep sleep, sure, but he felt—*uncertain.* Anxious, really, and it wasn't just nerves, he knew it. Anyone would be skitchy on their way to meet Church, but he was good at what he did and he didn't have much patience with idol worship. Besides, they shared the same rank . . .

He looked in the mirror again and shook his head. No time for this free-floating angst. He was a theoretical analyst, a man of science, over fifteen years in his field. Relying on gut feelings had kept him alive in the days of his warrior youth, but those days were long gone. The *Innominata* was a research station; he'd be using his instincts to figure out whether to have the soypro chicken or the soypro beef for lunch. And yet—

Yet nothing. He was going to be late.

Crespi straightened his shoulders and headed out for the bridge. The dimly lit corridor was empty and the ship had a deserted feel to it; except for the low hum of the air recycler, there was no sound, and the canned oxy was cold and dry, like the air in a tomb. Most of the crew would be in the mess hall, gulping coffee and trying to shake off the sleep, but for a few seconds, Crespi felt like he was the only living being on the transport, the last man in the universe. A fleeting trace of that anxiety again, monophobia perhaps . . .

He blinked, frowned. *What's this sole survivor shit? Next thing you're gonna want a night-light. It's those damn rumors, they're getting to you, too, just admit it.*

Maybe that *was* it, although someone would have to put a rifle to his head to make him say it out loud. Rumors were generally so much puffed air, and he had discredited the "vine" on the *Innominata* without hesitation. How many times had he heard phrases like "clandestine experiments" and "unreported deaths" in the past? In his line of work? Every year or so there was a rumble about some renegade scientist or top brasser who had gone mental and set up some bizarre operation, like the one about Doctor Reuf with the DNA pushing, or Spears's drone army. Pull the other one, it has bells.

On the other hand, he had never been assigned to any of those places. And Church's current setup was so hushed that Admiral Stevens didn't even know what he was up to, undoubtedly one of the reasons he had sent ol' by-the-book Crespi—to find out what skeletons Church had hiding up here and report back like a good little soldier . . .

Fuck it, he was going to find out soon enough. He rounded the curve in the passageway and stepped onto the bridge, the door sliding shut behind him.

The room was warm and smelled like boiled coffee. Heller and Shannon were at the com, in front of the window. Blake stood behind them, his arms resting on Shannon's chair, and they were all talking softly, their gazes focused on the station outside.

"Greetings, all," said Crespi, moving forward.

"Greetings, sir." That from Lieutenant Blake. The conversation between the three men died as Crespi joined them.

He studied the *Innominata* for a moment. Standard military research station, 700 series, a big one. He'd been on half a dozen just like it; multilab, could fit two hundred people, easy, although there were less than a hundred on board according to the reports. It loomed in front of them like a dark beacon, the dull glow from the landers barely illuminating the docking pad.

"So, that's she who cannot be named," he said quietly. He bent closer to the window to see past the large, fuzzy dice that someone (surely Heller) had hung above the console.

"Haven't you been before, sir?" Lieutenant Colonel Shannon glanced up at him, the lines of fatigue still clear around his eyes.

Crespi looked back at the station. "Nope, nope . . ." His new home, dark, cold—

Behind them, Blake cleared his throat in a contrived manner. Heller turned in his seat to face Crespi.

"Um, sir, I know we're not supposed to know what goes on there, but I was wondering if you could debunk some ugly rumors—"

Crespi stayed carefully neutral. "Rumors?"

Heller shot a glance at Blake and continued. "Well, sir . . ." and the rest, all in a rush, "well, we've heard that there are some kind of strange experiments going on, and that crew members are expendable there, that they're used in these tests—"

"That's enough, Heller. I wouldn't concern myself with rumors, if I were you. A man doesn't want to be known as a gossip."

It came out harsh, but he was suddenly annoyed by all of it, angry with his own anxiety. This wasn't a haunted house and they weren't kids; it was a goddamn science lab where Church was probably running an angle on plant intelligence or something as banal, some innocuous series of proofs on something distinctly *boring*.

Heller flushed and shot another look at Blake. It was silent for a few seconds, and then Shannon piped up helpfully.

"Coffee, sir?" He motioned toward the steaming dispenser to one side of the com.

Crespi shook his head and turned back toward the door. "No, thank you. See you at the landing, men."

"Yes, sir," they answered in unison, Heller's sullen voice lower than the rest.

Crespi stopped at the exit and turned for one final look at the *Innominata*, hanging alone in the emptiness. It was an ordinary research station, and that was all.

He walked out, repeating it firmly in his mind. *That's all.*

2

In her late teens, Sharon McGuinness had tried most of the synth drugs that her peers were into and had been unimpressed. They'd been fun for an experimentation stint, and she still didn't regret knowing what she'd been missing, but for the most part, being separated from organized thought for days at a time had gotten old real fast. Not to mention a few of her less stable acquaintances had developed actual habits and just faded away into unwashed cluelessness, a fate much worse than reality.

What she had hated even more than the loss of coherency had been the mornings after; crawling out of bed in the late afternoon with sticky teeth and a vague nausea, combined with a definite sense of brain death—it was, all in all, not a particularly attractive package . . .

And look at me now! All of the aftermath and none of the fun, 'cause I'm a grown-up!

Whee. McGuinness sat hunched over her thermos and waited for the scent of crappy instant coffee to do something for her brain. Six or seven of the guys milled around, grunting and shuffling in a postsleep trance. Like her, they had made their way to the mess hall ASAP, hoping that nourishment of some kind would help and knowing that it never did. Even the tepid shower had hardly been worth the effort, the recycled spray barely penetrating the numb fogginess.

". . . fuckin' age of neotechnology and nobody has come up with a decent cupa instant . . ." That from fellow Lieutenant Corey, said to no one in particular. The young officer stood by the dispenser looking like a rumpled zombie, eyes deeply circled by shadow.

Grunts from the grunts, and McGuinness smiled weakly in his direction. He had a point; she'd give her left tit for a double espresso.

Well, maybe.

Corey suddenly straightened up and managed a half-assed salute. "Sir!"

McGuinness turned her bleary gaze to the door and then started to stand, *officer on the deck*—

"At ease, all. As you were."

McGuinness slouched back down, wondering how the colonel did it. Crespi had been up as long as they had, but he looked crisp and wide awake, his deep voice strong and clear—like he'd just woken from a restful sleep. And then gone jogging.

Bastard.

The doctor studied their bleary faces as they settled back into their respective stupors. She didn't know Crespi well except by reputation; cold, precise, not a creative genius but relentless in his attention to detail—in other words, the perfect scientist. Not to mention as by-the-book Marine as they came. He had maybe ten TS on her, although it didn't show much—except for the lines of his face, he had the physique of a much younger man. His dark eyes were bright and sharp, set into his craggy features like hawk's eyes, missing nothing . . .

McGuinness snapped out of her weary musing as she realized that he was watching her in turn, a couple of meters in front of her table. He raised one eyebrow quizzically.

She cleared her throat. "Uh, I don't feel well, sir."

The colonel sat down in one of the molded chairs across from her. "Neither do I, McGuinness. In fact, I think I must feel as bad as you look."

A few raspy chuckles around the room. *Great.* Crespi wore the barest hint of a smirk.

"I—" She closed her mouth before it could get her into trouble and rolled her head back, stared at the plastiform ceiling. "Yes, sir. I'm feeling fine now, and I hope you soon will be, too."

This time, the snickers were disguised as minor coughing fits. McGuinness straightened her shoulders and looked at the colonel, who smiled openly now.

"No question, Lieutenant. Your recovery has been an inspiration to us all."

Well, at least he had *some* sense of humor. The others went back to their shuffling and monosyllabic conversations. McGuinness waited for Crespi to say something else, but he held silent, went back to watching the crew as they stumbled around aimlessly.

She felt a deep twinge in her gut, the tightening of a fist that had lain there for too long. It was time to find out what he knew.

She took a sip of the watery coffee and tried to sound uninterested in his answer. "Will I be working under you on board the *Innominata*, sir?"

Crespi turned his sharp gaze back to her. "Not likely, McGuinness, not if your luck holds. I expect to be deeply involved in some excruciatingly banal series tests."

Was it her imagination, or was that bantering tone a cover? The knot in her belly tightened. He was a tough read, but if she had to place bets, she'd say that he was as uninformed as the rest of them.

"Sounds good to me," she said, and looked away, continued with the feigned boredom. "The *Innominata* is a little too hush-hush, too 'didn't-happen never-was' to suit my taste."

Crespi leaned closer. "If that's the case, why did you volunteer for this tour?"

McGuinness shrugged. "Good question." *And you don't need to know the answer, sir.*

Several beats of silence. She finally glanced at him, noted the frown above those piercing eyes as he studied her face. He seemed about to say something else—

A voice crackled out over the com. "Colonel Doctor Crespi, sir. Colonel Thompson wishes to see you on the upper bridge before landing. Sir."

Crespi stared at her for another second, then looked away. "Very good."

He stood, nodded at her, and walked away from the table.

McGuinness sipped again from her thermos, relieved. He was quick, maybe *too* quick, but that might turn out to be an asset—

One of the men made some crack that she didn't quite hear, but she laughed along with the rest of them and stared down at her pale hands that suddenly trembled, ever so slightly . . .

3

Crespi stood on the landing deck of the *Innominata* and waited patiently, feeling a light sweat build up beneath his uniform cap in spite of the brisk air; goddamn covers were still made out of some synthwool blend. More than one soldier in full dress khaks had passed out on a hot day, probably too well trained to take their damn hat off—particularly not if they were waiting for a superior officer, and definitely not if that officer was an unknown . . .

"Colonel Doctor Crespi? I'm Admiral Thaves."

Crespi straightened his shoulders as a short, barrel-chested man walked on deck, calling out to him across the floor. His booming voice reverberated through the high-ceilinged room, as direct and impatient as his heavy stride.

Crespi snapped a salute, held it. "Colonel Doctor Anthony Crespi reporting for duty, sir."

As Thaves got closer, Crespi studied him discreetly; the admiral looked nothing like he had pictured. He had heard that Thaves had been a field man for most of his career, but the figure in front of him was soft-looking, his grayed, wavy hair styled slickly back. He *did* have that old-boy air Crespi associated with ancient war holovids, stiff posture in spite of the paunch—but it appeared that the last action Thaves had seen was decades past.

On the other hand, the admiral's face looked like it had been in every battle waged in the last fifty TS—weathered and lined, cheeks going to jowl. His nose had been broken at least once and badly reset, and was as red as a rotten beet. The burst capillaries spoke of too many four-star martinis.

Thaves stepped in front of him and then smiled, his teeth even but stained. Crespi caught a faint scent of cigars and hair oil. The admiral clapped him on the shoulder as if they were old friends, reunited after years apart.

"At ease until further notice, Crespi. Welcome aboard the *Innominata.*" He nodded, grinned wider. "You must have some very influential friends back home—a lot of good men were in line for this post."

Thaves turned and started back for the lander door without waiting for an answer. Crespi sighed inwardly and fell in behind him.

"No influential friends that I'm aware of, sir," he said, careful to keep his tone neutral. "My experience with—"

"No nepotism implied, Doctor," Thaves cut him off, held up one meaty hand without even turning to look at him. "Your record speaks for itself. Much sub rosa, eh?"

The older man's manner was jovial, but Crespi had the definite impression that Thaves was putting on an act, doing the dance that the brass often seemed to do when *they* were put up against an unknown. Apparently he was aware that Crespi had been sent for more than one reason—but how much did Thaves think he knew?

He tried again. "Well, to a certain extent, sir. Intelligence was never my strong—"

"Yes, most impressive, a good theoretical analyst is always valuable." Thaves finally glanced back at him, grin still in place. "Colonel Doctor Church may well find a use for you."

Thaves turned and walked forward again, leading them through the wide mechanical door and into a quiet corridor. Military issue, right down to the dark plasticrete wall panels and crappy baseboard heaters. Very inexpensive, and it showed; cracks and chips of the cheap material dotted the bare floor, mostly around the heating units—they eroded the walls and kept the air in the hall nice and chilly.

The atmosphere of this part of the station left something to be desired; the air was recycled, smelled faintly of disinfectant and sweat, and had that strange, flat taint of overuse; Crespi had grown accustomed to it through the years, but somehow it seemed worse than usual.

Terrific. And if he recalled the layout properly, they were headed toward officers' quarters . . .

So what was the game? Besides the fact that the admiral kept interrupting him, he implied that Crespi was NI, that he'd come to dig for dirt. Obviously the man thought he was more in the loop than he actually was—which *could* be an asset, depending on how much leeway he could get from it . . .

"Of course, I expect to be working closely with Colonel Doctor Church."

The admiral kept walking, and his response was mumbled in an overly pleasant and distinctly patronizing tone. "Well, nothing is carved in stone . . ."

Enough. Crespi frowned, and stepped up to walk alongside the admiral. "Sir, I hope there hasn't been a misunderstanding. My assignment is to succeed Colonel Doctor Lennox as Colonel Doctor Church's research partner."

They turned another corner in the hallway, and Thaves motioned to the first in a row of doors, grin in place. "There's your quarters, A89. There's a briefing card in the player. Get familiar with the floor, your orderly is on call—"

"Admiral Thaves, I *am* here to work with Colonel Doctor Church, am I not?"

They had stopped in front of his quarters and now faced each other, Crespi looking down on the stocky admiral. Thaves still smiled, but there was something else in his eyes, an aw-shucks look that didn't sit well on his scarred face.

"That has to be worked out. Why don't you brief yourself and have your orderly show you around? We have a lounge that might surprise you, quite a—"

"I would prefer to meet with Colonel Doctor Church and get brought up to speed right away, sir."

The admiral smiled wider, only it didn't look particularly pleasant anymore. It was almost painful, like he was trying to get every tooth into the act, to convince the doctor just how *reasonable* he was being.

"Crespi, you have at your disposal the biggest research area on this station. You'll have plenty of time to set up and run any operation you want. For now, though, why don't you relax?"

"Shit-eating," that's the term. *Shit-eating grin.* Crespi was almost dumbfounded at the man's ability to avoid a direct answer.

Thaves went on, the grin turning to a conspiratorial leer. "Perhaps you'll find this a bit blunt, but I've found that a little boy-girl action takes the edge off a long, cold sleep. Or, you know, whatever suits your fancy. Now, up in the lounge you'll find—"

"To be a bit blunt myself, sir, all I want to do is meet Colonel Doctor Church and get to work."

To be honest, he was also quite tempted to beat the admiral's head in with his briefcase—though that would probably seem imprudent at this early juncture.

Too bad.

Thaves sighed. "Well, I'm sorry to have to inform you that Church has determined that he doesn't need a new second in command. But don't worry, you'll have the best research team that we can muster, I mean that, we'll—"

Crespi's hands had clenched into fists. He didn't have a particularly quick temper, never with superiors, but this pug-nosed good ol' boy had pushed it as far as it would go.

"Sir, I respectfully request that I meet with Colonel Doctor Church *immediately!*"

Not one ruffled feather. Thaves shrugged and held out his hands almost apologetically. "Oh, well. Request denied."

Crespi glowered down at him, angrier than he'd

been in a long time, almost ready to punch that
smarmy little smile through the back of the admiral's
head—

Deep breath, Tony.

Right. Crespi slowly unfurled his fingers, one, both
hands. Pickman was backing him, and Pickman had a
lot more clout than this man. There was no need for
this.

Crespi lowered his tone, took another deep breath.
"Admiral Thaves, I have my assignment and I intend
to carry it out. If I have to petition superseding authority to do so, I will."

Finally the grin was gone, wiped off clean, and for
the first time Crespi saw some of what had gotten
Thaves to his rank. The admiral drew himself to full
height and there was a steely coolness in his gaze.

"Oh, my golly. A tough guy. Isn't that fine?" Sarcas-
tic, but at least no longer patronizing. "Why don't you
go relax in your quarters while I go discuss this with
Colonel Doctor Church?"

Thaves scowled up at him, waited. Crespi saluted
dutifully. "Sir."

His commanding officer turned and stalked away,
back down the corridor. Crespi opened the door to
his new home and threw his briefcase across the
room.

4

hurch sat at his bare desk and gently ran his finger over and across the com switch. The softest touch from his nimble fingers; a caress, really, not enough for the primitive console to even acknowledge. Bare desk in a bare room, except for a few buttons set into the monitor that connected him to the rest of the station . . .

He sighed, then punched one long finger at the switch. It was time to meet the great, unheard-of Crespi who had caused Thaves so much disease.

"Yes?"

Poor Admiral Thaves, such desperation in that one word!

"Alright. Send him down."

"Fine, fine." The man's relief was obvious although

23

he tried to hide it. "I think this will work out fine, Doctor; I agree with your decision—"

"Very well," he said, and hit discom before he had to hear any more of the admiral's false bluster. He wasn't particularly concerned, but Thaves seemed to be half-hysterical over the new man's arrival and it paid to placate the man. The admiral needed his delusion of authority, though he'd been in Church's pocket for years—a fact that everyone on board accepted, just as they accepted Thaves's blindness to it. The admiral ran the station efficiently and left him alone, and Church wanted it to stay that way. Though if this Crespi was even half as good as Thaves seemed to think, he might actually be useful . . .

And wouldn't that be a pleasant change?

Truly, to have a peer aboard! It had been too long, days, weeks, months—he'd lost track, really. There were probably only a handful of people in the known universe who could even *begin* to comprehend his work, let along appreciate the implications; indeed, perhaps fewer—the nature of scientific study was reclusive at best, the chance to meet with others in the field as rare as hen's teeth. He usually didn't mind, as much of humanity seemed to tend toward boring; lately, though, he'd longed for the company of an associate, a rival mind if not an equal . . .

The annoying bleat of the door buzzer disturbed his thoughts. Damned thing should be disconnected, or at least tuned to something more pleasant. Church sighed again and went to greet his visitor.

He opened the door to a tall, rather stern-looking man in his early forties, dark hair in a standard military buzz. His features seemed sharp, almost angry-looking, the etched furrows in his brow suggesting a man who didn't laugh often.

How funny!

"Colonel Doctor Crespi? I'm Paul Church. Won't you come in?"

He stepped back, ushered Crespi in with a wave.

"Thanks," said Crespi. Gruff voice. Polite enough, though somewhat strained. Apparently Thaves had rattled the boy's cage a bit too hard.

He turned, motioned at the one uncomfortable seat bolted to the floor in front of his desk. "Please, sit down."

"Thanks."

Marvelous manners, his mother was undoubtedly quite proud; time, though, to find out what he was made of.

"Pleasant journey?" Church waited for the doctor to seat himself and then sat down across from him.

Crespi half smiled. "Uneventful as only cold sleep can be."

"No, I didn't mean your trip. I mean the months ahead. Shall they be pleasant—or otherwise?"

Crespi didn't answer but studied him carefully, unable to keep the wariness out of his gaze. At least the man thought before he spoke—a far cry from Admiral Thaves.

Church waited, but Crespi seemed caught up in his scrutiny, searching for the most appropriate response to such a presumptuous question. Ah, but he *did* miss intelligent company! With David gone there was no one worth even talking to anymore, his efforts wasted on the sluggards that infested the *Innominata* ...

Unfortunately, time was too short to play innuendo games with his new guest, as much fun as they could be. He'd have to get to the point and see how this Crespi operated.

"Things are pretty well established in their course here, Crespi. It's all routine at this point. It wasn't necessary for you to be sent to replace Lennox. In fact, I took steps to prevent it."

He smiled gently at that now open wariness and went on. "If he hadn't died when he did, he would have been transferred. Nothing for him to do here. Nothing for you to do, either."

He leaned back in the stiff chair, hands behind his head, keeping his tone as friendly and bored as possible.

Here we go!

"My research has been downsized. Hardly enough to keep me engaged, really. Space-borne virus typing, dull stuff."

His gaze fixed on Crespi, waiting to see which way he'd jump. Church figured on anger, although there was always the placating, diplomatic approach . . .

Crespi stood, placed his hands on the desk, and leaned forward, glowering. "I understand that one of your 'viruses' pushed Colonel Doctor Lennox's brain out of the back of his head."

Angry but delivered well, cool and quiet instead of the expected bravado. Obviously the good doctor felt that he carried some kind of clout—an admiral's ear, perhaps? Or some other—extremity?

Church tittered. "Oh, no, Crespi. What a macabre notion—viruses are little teeny things."

Crespi leaned farther across the desk. "Church, my tolerance for baloney is practically nil. If you won't shoot straight with me, you can explain why to a board of review."

My, how—authoritative!

"The other boys won't play fair and now you're going to go call dad." He smiled wider to show that he wasn't truly offended. "Honestly, I'm disappointed by your lack of resourcefulness."

Crespi continued to scowl. Humorless, utterly humorless.

Church stopped smiling and stood up himself, suddenly tired by the game. "You're out of your league, Crespi. Your superiors have tossed you into the *Innominata* like cave men throwing a dog into a pond to catch their reflections."

No response except that sharp and angry face. Very *masculine* of him. He'd just have to work around Crespi for the time being, a nuisance but apparently the only way to get back to the research. Perhaps he could take over some of the busywork that David used to occupy himself with while Church decided what to do with him.

"Well, come on, let's go." He smiled anew. "I'll show you my setup."

They walked toward the door, some of the tension easing out of Crespi's features. They stepped into the dim corridor and Church pointed them toward G Lab, noting how high Crespi held his shoulders, a look of authority to every movement.

This might actually be interesting.

Paul Church was definitely *not* what he had expected. They walked down the corridor side by side, the smaller man barely coming up to Crespi's shoulders and with the look of a genius eccentric—too thin, long, dirty white hair receding back from his high forehead, smudged glasses, a baggy sweatshirt beneath his lab coat.

It wasn't the look so much as the distinctly odd attitude. Very offhand, almost indifferent—yet somehow he got the feeling that Church was toying with him, or at least thought that he was.

Well. He had his orders, even if it required that he be patronized by the mysterious Church. He'd stewed in his quarters for a good twenty minutes before Thaves had given him the go-ahead, which obviously meant that Church had okayed it. If it took a little game playing, so be it. Results were what mattered.

They approached a lab door with two heavily armed guards in front; they both wore heavyweight battle armor, an updated version of the stuff he had worn in the field. High-impact acid resist, even the headgear. Both soldiers carried full auto rifle/incinerators, the kind they used to clean out infestations . . .

Crespi didn't want to think about that.

Church smiled at the two men. "O'Hara, Lawless. This is Colonel Doctor Crespi, he'll be working with me in G Lab."

Crespi acknowledged their salutes with a nod. Who the hell were they guarding against? "I'll need to be put on the bioscan ASAP, of course."

"Hmm?" Church touched one bony finger to the imprint pad and then entered a brief clearance code. "Oh, there's no hurry. We'll see how things turn out."

Crespi grit his teeth to keep from screaming. The heavy door slid open and Church stepped into a short hall leading to what was presumably the lab entrance. Church waited until the door slid shut before he spoke.

"Let me remind you, Church, that you are not my superior officer. All this lateral obstruction is going to serve you very poorly." *And it's gonna frustrate me into a heart attack to boot.*

Church opened the second door and then smiled pleasantly over his shoulder. "Can you still get good chocolate on Earth? I heard they'd stopped making it."

Jesus, who did he have to kill to get a straight answer? What *was* this place? It couldn't be a *military* station, there were rules and regs on *those*, and what was so goddamn secret that every sentence he spoke had to be rephrased for him, to insure that he wouldn't presume to do his *job*?

He scowled, but followed Church into the facility, his shoes squeaking faintly against the polished plasticrete. They stood on a small, raised platform in a huge room, perhaps two meters above the main floor. Four or five low-level techs were scattered about, a couple of them working at a computer console that took up an entire side of the vast chamber. The place stank of industrial-grade disinfectant.

"You have one hell of a lot of nerve, Church—"

"I accept the compliment, Crespi." The old scientist walked to the end of the ramp and looked down over the rail into some kind of sunken enclosure.

Crespi stared around, amazed. What was going on here, armed guards and secret access codes? There was no virus typing going on here; it looked more like a war zone.

"How long did you think you could get away with this?" He motioned about, feeling more perplexed than he had so far all day.

Church looked away from the rail, his expression

almost apologetic. "Have you ever had to testify against a personal friend? I couldn't make myself do it."

"What are you—"

Crespi smiled amiably, then pointed down over the railing.

"Look."

Crespi walked forward and looked into the enclosure—

And felt his heart begin to hammer in his chest as a cold sweat broke out all over his body.

"Shhh, don't wake him," whispered Church, but Crespi barely registered the words. Below them, crouched in one corner of the heated pen, was an adult drone. Its malignant dark sheen seemed to swallow up the dim light that bathed the chamber, and as Crespi leaned over, the creature's long, black head shifted up to face them, its tail coiling loosely around the hard, metallic body.

If Church said anything more, he missed it. Because even though his gaze never left the drone, Crespi was suddenly over a million miles away.

5

Sergeant Crespi yawned, careful to hide it from Captain Wilcox and the rest of the crew. He hadn't slept much the night before and the rolling transport seemed to have a lulling effect in spite of the rough ground. He was second in com after Wilcox, at least on board the armored vehicle, and restless nights were no excuse for dragging ass— especially in front of the captain, a gung-ho type if ever there was.

Restless, now there was an understatement. A conversation and a few drinks with Cady Trask had led to a longer discussion in her quarters—which had led to several very pleasant hours of no talking at all. He glanced around at some of the other noncoms, stifled another yawn. Corporal Trask caught his gaze and smiled before discreetly looking away, her dark red hair pulled loosely beneath her helmet. She didn't look tired at all; amazing. And just the tiniest bit— disappointing?

God, I wasn't that bad, was I?

Crespi wasn't much of a player, never had been—he hadn't spent his youth chasing after sexual gratification, which usually seemed to be more trouble than it was worth ... but he liked to think that his prowess wasn't *horribly* lacking. Adequate at the very least. It was just that his work always seemed to come first, always had—

Trask, though. She was something. Bright, funny, attractive—and she was working toward a career in engineering, particularly biotech stuff. Maybe when this little stint was over he'd find out where she was going to station next ...

The transport lurched to a halt in the multileveled cave. Crespi blinked his eyes, sat up straighter. There were eleven others in the group, not including Wilcox and his two sweepers. The captain had apparently witnessed battle with this breed before, though none of the other grunts and noncoms had actually *seen* an alien drone, except in vids. Himself included. They had been brought together for the occasion, to get some experience in the field; most were working on some aspect of bioanalysis or other, and the Corps seemed to think it was important for them to be there, firsthand experience and all. Rumor had it that there would be some fast promotions for those choosing to specialize in drone research, although the higher-ups hadn't seen fit to fill in the blanks. These creatures were supposed to be the newest up-and-coming threat to mom and apple pie ... right. It was always something.

Well, they can't be that *deadly, sending us in.* Crespi rolled his head against his chest, uncomfortable in the light armor. Precautionary equipment, armed and ready, yadayadayada. Wilcox had spent a lot of time talking about how nasty these creatures were, but he seemed confident that they were just here to watch. Swell; months of work wasted to come to some no-name planetoid and witness the slaughter of a few big bugs.

The captain stood and faced the crew. "Alright, people. Regulations say you're here as backup for the lead team and to provide a retreat escort if necessary." He cleared his throat, smiled somewhat smugly. It looked strange on his thin, lined face.

"What you're *really* going to do is sit back, relax, and watch Rupp and Hollister liquefy every alien in this cavern."

Wilcox motioned at his two sweepers, standing stiffly behind him. Now *they* looked like aliens—fully armored in what looked like silver-plated freeze units, their faces dim behind thick, tinted plexi. Each of them held two of the latest in military tech, particle-plasma projectors. The heavy weapons rode on the outsides of their arms, fully sheathed and mean-looking, basically handheld rocket launchers—only each one emitted a coherent beam of charged particles. Crespi had seen prototype tests; stand in the way and become soup du jour.

The back of the transport slid up and out, letting the humid, foul-smelling air of the cavern breeze across their faces. Christ, that stank! The air had the thick, warm feel of rot, like badly decayed matter. Cloying.

The vehicle's outside lights cast a good ten meters

of glow, exposing bare rocky walls that seemed too shiny, slick. Must be a leak from above ground, that'd explain the humidity—but that *smell*, that was unprecedented.

Wilcox addressed the two men in the heavy suits. "Make it a clean sweep, men. I want this place sterilized."

"Aye-aye, sir," said one of them, the crackle of his voice over the com sounding strangely muted, hollow. The two of them stepped out of the back and into the cavern's gloom.

Crespi leaned forward to see better. The men moved carefully, their thick boots thudding heavily against the cave floor. Each movement sent echoes through the still darkness, the only other sound that of their amplified breathing.

When they were maybe five or six meters away, one of them (Hollister?) spoke quickly.

"Over there!"

A sudden clatter of sound, claws on stone. And what sounded like a low, guttural hiss—

There were three of them, huge, black. They crouch-jumped into the circle of light cast by the transport, long, slick heads and chittering jaws, dripping—

Twin beams of brilliant matter flooded the blackness, joined by the grinding *thrum* of the particle projectors. A third and fourth ray as Rupp fired. The creatures couldn't have know what hit them as their dark limbs exploded backward in a hail of sizzling acid, their scaled bodies crumpling down.

The rock behind them burned, the smoke pungent, chemical.

"Mother of God," someone half whispered behind Crespi.

"Offhand, I'd say this represents the end of the alien threat—"

"No shit, Sherlock—"

Crespi couldn't take his eyes off of the smoldering rocks and the dismembered—*things* that lay in front of them. His body felt frozen, as if his blood had been replaced by liquid nitrogen. The soldiers behind him muttered and laughed in various states of awe, but Crespi felt something akin to terror. Monsters. They were *scientists*, what the fuck had they been sent into? Most of them hadn't ever been in combat, hadn't even used their boot-camp skills since before graduation, years past. Marines, yes, but trained fighters? Not them, not *any* of them, not anymore. Without even thinking about it he reached for his weapon, rested one cold hand against the butt.

Dazed, he glanced away for a second, saw Captain Wilcox staring out at the dead drones, a strange smile affixed to thin lips.

"Kinda takes all the sport right out of it, don't it?" Wilcox said, his eyes lit up from within.

Oh, shit . . . Crespi felt it, deep in his gut. This was bad, code red time, these things were fucking *lethal*—

Hollister and Rupp had moved out of the line of sight, off to one side of the ATV. All at once the hissing of the melting slag grew louder, more intense.

That's not slag—

The sweepers' voices blared out over the com, confident and excited. "Whoa, looks like the mother lode!"

"Get 'em all before they scatter!"

A flash and several low hums, and this time there

were inhuman shrieks of something like rage, high and shrill, so loud that it would take dozens, maybe *hundreds* of the things to make that much noise—

Hissing, acid on rocks now, the smoke pouring into the small transport at an incredible rate. Wilcox jumped forward, slammed his hand into the rear door control. Just before it came down, Crespi saw a flood of the viscous acid wash across the stone floor toward the transport.

He snapped his head around, caught Cady's horrified gaze, saw the sudden fear on the faces of the others. The projectors buzzed on, again and again, the smoke thickened—

"Hollister!" Rupp, his voice panicked.

"I can't see! I can't see!"

The ATV suddenly crashed to one side. Several of the crew cried out in alarm as Rupp and Hollister began to shout.

"The stuff's getting in! The fumes are getting *in*, the concentration is too much, I can't *breathe*—"

"The transport! The wheels, they're melting!"

That much acid—Crespi jumped up, pushed his way to the front of the ATV. From outside came the horrible alien screams, so many now, the projectors almost silent in their wake.

Wilcox shouted, "Crespi! Blow the bolts on the escape hatch!"

"Yessir!"

The hatch popped outward and a new flood of smoke pushed into Crespi's face from above. He drew his weapon, a handheld automatic machine pistol, and crawled out into the swimming darkness.

Behind him, Wilcox screamed, "Fight! Fight! Kill them, Marines!"

Crespi spun, searched for the two sweepers beneath the fog of burning rock. There, three o'clock, one down—

—and crouched over him was a nightmare vision, the blackness come to life. Easily three and a half meters tall, an impossible-looking thing made from ebony metal and stainless steel. A long, spined tail whip-cracked the air behind it, splashed through the ankle-deep pool of corrosive blood.

Bodies of so many creatures all around, parts and pieces of shattered limbs and exploded skulls. And there were more, alive and drooling, creeping out of the smoky shadows—

Shots fired all around Crespi as the others clambered onto the roof and found targets. Crespi sighted the monster on top of the fallen sweeper, squeezed the trigger again and again—

The fumes were almost blinding, searing Crespi's throat and nostrils. Hollister fired blindly into the oncoming creatures, spraying more acid across the cavern. Crespi heard human screams behind him as the blood flew, spattered onto unprotected flesh—

Out of nowhere, one of the drones leapt forward, grabbing Hollister from behind, its long, chitinous arms wrapped around him—and then its metal jaws shot forward, ripping the man's throat out through his spine in a gout of red.

"They've got Hollister!"

Wilcox screamed, barely audible in the din. "They've got *all* of us, you dumb sonuvabitch! Fight! *Fight!*"

More drones leapt out, ran for the transport through the waves of gore. Their blood splashed up, more of it flying and spitting across human skin.

Crespi was dizzy, ejected and jammed another mag into his weapon, turned in time to see one of the men fall off the roof and into the acid. The sounds of weaponfire were being drowned out by screams now, as a second, Corporal Chan, plummeted into the mire.

"Mother, I need help—"

Crespi fired again, turned and saw Tom Olsen, his hands clenched around his bleeding gut. Olsen staggered past and collapsed, the tips of his bloody ribs beginning to sizzle and melt. Private Olsen, his friend, dead—

The drones were falling, dying, but even through the dark smoke Crespi could see more of them coming, climbing over black bodies to get at the transport.

"Merciful Buddha, nooo—"

"I'm dead! I'm dead!"

Crespi spun, his bullets ripped into one of the things as it landed on the roof. He had time to see the man or woman whose face was melting, a pulpy bubbling mass of red. He saw Corporal Akely firing, suddenly falling, a long talon coming out of his gut, the monster clawing through his torso. Fourteen Marines, and now there were four, maybe five—

The cries of the alien drones were louder than the gunfire now.

Crespi screamed to no one as he jammed another magazine into his pistol. "Hopeless! This is hopeless!"

"Keep firing!" Wilcox, somewhere behind him, though Crespi could no longer see where. Tears ran from his scalded eyes, almost impossible to see anything—

"Tony—?"

At the sound of his name he stopped, spun—

And saw Cady Trask, crouched down, looking up at him almost calmly. Her red hair was down now, the helmet gone, her face pale and ethereal in the smoky gloom.

Her right arm was gone, the stump of her shoulder hissing and bubbling red foam. Blood trickled down from her mouth where she had bitten through her lower lip in shock and pain.

She stared at him for a scant second that seemed like an eternity—and then was jerked away by a long, spiny arm, pulled down into the mass of acid and limbs.

"NO!" Crespi blasted the creature as it disappeared into the haze—hoping to God that his bullets got to her before its teeth did . . .

There was a sudden, wrenching *crack* that assaulted all of his sense. The ATV lurched, slanted downward, sent another grunt to his acid death.

"What's happening?!" Crespi shouted.

Wilcox sent a hail of fire into a leaping drone. "The ledge is going! It's—"

The rest was lost in another deafening crunch. Crespi's thoughts raced, bleary and sick, *multilevel caves—*

"Grab something, ride it down, *stay on top!*"

Crespi fell, looped one arm through a metal strut, still clutching his gun—as the world spun away with a last rumbling *crack*, sending the tiny vehicle downward through space and into a void.

6

Crespi braced himself for the impact, eyes clenched shut, held on to the thick strut with all his strength. The weighted transport plummeted through the dark for a few impossibly long seconds, while all around he heard the screams of the creatures following them down.

BAMM!

The impact dislocated his shoulder and slammed his head into the metal paneling hard enough to blur his vision even further. There was no time to do it gently—he jerked his arm out and up, his teeth grit against the pain as the bone and muscle popped back into place.

Rocks and debris rained down from above, clattered in echo across the cave floor, joined only by bursts of static from the ruined ATV. The air was clearer here; muffled shafts of light struggled through a crevice to his left.

Something else struggled, too. A half-crushed drone, there in a pile of shattered rock.

Crespi slid from the slanted roof of the battered ATV and aimed. Squeezed. And watched as the alien's bizarre, twisted form exploded, bubbled into stillness.

Another sound, behind him, soft in the ringing aftermath of the shots. Crespi spun, pointed—

Sergeant Karl Gibbs crawled out from behind the transport, coughing, a gun in hand. He stood, stumbled over to Crespi. The look of fear seemed out of place on his strong features, the tension bunching his huge shoulders; Gibbs pumped iron, old style, had chatted with Crespi about it a few days before . . .

Crespi shook his head of the random thoughts, unable to focus. *This is impossible, didn't happen* couldn't *happen! They were Marines, for chrissake!*

For a moment they surveyed the wreckage all around them, the torn, hissing pieces of drone bodies—and the mostly unidentifiable remains of the Marines who had gone down with them. Crespi saw Wilcox, could only tell by the uniform; there was a thick slab of rock where his head should have been. He didn't want to look, didn't want to see Cady or Tom or any of them, not like this—

From somewhere out of the darkness beyond them, he heard a sound that his mind rejected, that he wanted to be an illusion more than he'd ever wanted anything. He checked the counter on his piece. Three rounds. *Three.*

Hissing. Talons on rocks.

"Fuck!" Gibbs stumbled over to Wilcox's corpse and snatched the captain's gun out of his limp hand.

Crespi looked around desperately, saw only rocks and death.

From the useless transport came another buzz of static, the transmission lost through the layers of rock. "ATV103, come— What's—in there—"

Crespi ran to the crushed door of the vehicle, screamed toward the stuttering intercom. "Code Red, they're coming! Get us out of here! Code Red!"

Gibbs shouted behind him. "Crespi!"

He searched for a weapon, nowhere, no time, ran back to see Gibbs fire at the first drone. Another one behind it, taken down in a blast of fire and acid. A third—

Crespi aimed carefully, felt no relief as his last three rounds shattered the shrieking monster. There were more coming, but they were farther behind, a few seconds, maybe the last few seconds of his life—

The ATV's com squawked amid the fading reverberations and the sounds of the drone pack moving closer.

"—not compromise the safety—" static, "out in the open, over?"

Shitshitshit! They wouldn't, *couldn't* come in, they were fucked!

"Crespi! Grenade left!"

He turned, saw Gibbs throw a six-second thermal at the light-filled crack in the cavern wall. Crespi dropped his useless weapon as he scrambled over a pile of rocks to crouch behind the transport, Gibbs right behind him.

A horrible scream behind them. Gibbs turned, fired at the metallic blackness that ran toward them—

WHOOOM!

A deafening explosion filled the cavern as the grenade blew, rocks and dust flying. The ATV rocked and swayed, settled. Crespi felt liquid trickle from one ear and from his nose, barely registered the sudden silence before Gibbs was pulling at him, jerking at his arm.

They stumbled through the settling cloud of powdered rock and then Gibbs was climbing and pulling him up.

"Come on—" The barest whisper, though Gibbs must have shouted it.

Oh, God, daylight. A sudden wistful hope filled his fogged brain. They were out, crawling through the jagged hole the grenade had left, halfway up a barren slope in a series of barren slopes. Crespi squinted down into the shadows, saw dark shapes moving toward them—

Gibbs pushed him, hard, and then they were both falling, rolling down the steep hill and away from the hole where the monsters dwelt. Crespi felt a rib break, then another, and he cried out—but at least there was light, at least they weren't in the cavern anymore.

He slid to a stop, saw that Gibbs was near. The sergeant was pointing, shouting. "Come on, we can make it!"

Crespi looked, saw what Gibbs was pointing at. The ship. The beautiful transport ship that would get them the fuck away from this nightmare . . .

Run, they had to run. The ship wouldn't come any closer, only a few hundred meters, they could make it—

Crespi stood, looked back—and saw several glistening black shapes, no less frightening in the daylight, creeping out of the rip in the stone. They were coming.

Gibbs saw what he was looking at and started to run, limping. Crespi took a few steps and then fell, got up and kept going in spite of the terrible pain, ribs, shoulder, his entire body; hell was behind them.

He didn't look back, kept his bleary gaze on the ship in front of them. Gibbs was faster in spite of the limp, but they both moved slow, too slow. The ship hovered, kicking up whirling clouds of dust far ahead.

Crespi didn't hear it because of the ringing in his ears, but he knew, suddenly knew—something was right behind him. Something much faster than him.

A bolt of agonizing pain in his side as a giant, dark claw grasped his broken ribs. He was spun around, vaguely aware that he screamed but unable to hear the depths of terror in his own voice when he saw the thing that held him.

A giant, seething animal, crowned with a massive, gleaming comb of black. She had two pairs of arms, the ones that held him long and articulated with tight strips of dark matter, the talons sharp and piercing. Blood ran from the wounds in his chest, and he saw behind her another entrance to the hellish cavern— her lair. For this monstrosity was surely the queen, half again as tall as her drone minions, hissing and screaming at him with no sound—

She brought him closer, close enough to see the pearly spittle glisten across her steel teeth. The horrible jaws opened, impossibly wide, and he saw the second set extend, slowly, so slowly—

Crespi struggled, screamed, his dusty boots kicking against her skull, but she was too strong, carried him to her dripping jaws with ease. He was going to die.

—I'm sorry, sorry—

Suddenly she jerked, screamed, and even through the ringing he could hear the bullets, see the splashes of bubbling blood that exploded from her back and pattered the dust beyond them. Her tremendous hands clenched, crushed him—

—and dropped him to the ground. She turned, shrieked in rage and hurt—and then fell, writhing, pulling herself away from him, back to her darkness. Miraculously, only a few tiny droplets of her obscene blood had hit him, splashing across his chest armor.

Hands clutched at him, unbuckled the hissing chest plate and threw it aside. Gibbs. "You all right?!"

He was being pulled again, and he let out a strangled sob; he was alive, hurting but alive. "No—"

Gibbs slung Crespi's arm over his shoulder and limped on, grunting with each shuffling step. "We gotta get in the clear so they'll open the lock, we're gonna make it, hold on—"

It seemed an eternity of rocks and dust beneath their feet, and Crespi could hear the sound of the ship's air compressors getting louder—but behind them, the shrieks of the creatures also increased in volume. Gibbs kept talking, mumbling words of encouragement. Crespi realized that he was in shock, for in spite of the planetoid's desert temperature, he was shaking with cold.

It was Gibbs's laughter that finally made him look up. In front of them, not five meters, the drop lock of the transport ship, lowered within their reach. Gibbs let go for the barest second, hoisted himself up onto the grided platform, and then reached back for Crespi.

The large man lifted him easily and pushed him

ahead, over the waist-high railing and into the lock. Crespi still shook, but he managed a smile in return to Gibbs's wide grin, reaching back with numb arms to help. The ship lifted, up and away, the desert rock dwindling beneath them at incredible speed.

God, they were safe! They had made it, alive, and Crespi began to laugh as Gibbs grinned, the truth of it in his eyes.

And then the grin opened wider, the eyes suddenly bulging from their sockets. Gibbs screamed, his thick fingers clutching convulsively through the wire, skin cracking—

NO!

A dark metal rod, red and slick, tipped with gnashing teeth, shot out from Gibb's open mouth. His cracked skull elongated, ripped in half, spewed Crespi with warm, quivering flesh and blood. The sergeant reached forward with one dying hand, a last instinct to save himself—and fell away, the alien still enmeshed in his body, its inner jaws clicking wetly through the back of his skull. He tumbled down in a cloud of his own gore, into the teeming nest of black drones far below that hissed and shrieked their fury to the skies.

Crespi fell to his knees, the hot wind whispering past his tortured ears. Fell to his side, curled into a ball of aches and wounds. And finally, he slept.

7

Church watched as Doctor Crespi's face went pale and his eyes seemed to glaze over with some ancient dream, a nightmare by the expression. Interesting; perhaps they were kindred spirits, at least in shared experience. Or perhaps some little drone had jumped out at him from behind a rock on some piddling mission or other, frightened poor Crespi into soiling his skivvies. Traumatic, to be sure . . .

Church gazed back down at the now-sleeping drone, felt a trace of a smile tug at the corners of his mouth. Sometimes things came full circle; how fortunate that he was here to appreciate the irony of it.

He blinked, and in that briefest flash of darkness, he remembered. Not the specifics, the sounds or smells, but the *feeling*—of knowing the hatred for flesh, the silent screaming realized in the separation of body and spirit—

Another blink and it was gone. Below them, the beast hissed softly, asleep in its own dark reality. And now Church *did* smile, feeling a sudden rush of something like affection for the creature. After all, *he* was no longer in a cage.

Doctor Crespi had gone positively numb in flashback, so Church politely cleared his throat before speaking.

"Won't you let this spunky little fellow into your heart?"

Crespi's eyes seemed to clear a bit, but he was still quite ashen. "What—what if it—it can't jump out?"

Church shook his head. "Don't worry. There's a force field, of course. And the pit is seven meters deep, with no purchase—solid acid-neutralizing alloy."

Crespi didn't look convinced, his gaze steady on the drone. Church pointed at one of the dozen electrodes set low into the walls of the enclosure. "See the electrodes? They're motion-activated. If an alien attempted to jump, it would be roasted alive."

They stood and watched for a moment, but the napping creature didn't stir. Church turned and walked back up the ramp, stopping at the metal steps when he realized Crespi hadn't followed.

"Colonel Doctor Crespi?"

The man seemed to shake himself, then backed away from the viewing platform to join him.

Church led him down the stairs and onto the main floor, over to the vid console. He tapped a few keys at a small screen, pulling up a layout grid for the lab connections.

"This will give you an idea of the extent of this operation."

Crespi studied the map, frowning thoughtfully. "This must utilize half the *Innominata*'s nonrenewable resources."

Church smiled. "More like five-eighths."

When Crespi looked up, he was still frowning, but some color had come back into his face. "Why are you so eager to help me shut you down?"

Church leaned past him, tapped a few more keys, then motioned up to the vid screen as it flared to life. "Ask me later. Heads up."

The screen contained a close-up shot of the sleeping drone, the shielded camera illuminating the creature in full, glorious color. Church smiled again; he had to admit, he liked this part.

He punched the small yellow button at his fingertip and the drone sprang awake, screaming.

Crespi's heart plummeted into his stomach as the horrible shriek echoed dully through the lab. The picture on the giant screen was one of pure rage, the alien leaping to its guard, arms outstretched and ready to destroy. Its long tail whipped around, lashed into the walls of the pit in a flurry of metallic slaps; its jaws dripped ichor as it spun, searching for its tormentor. Church had shocked it, hard.

He couldn't keep the tremor from his voice. "Why did you do that?"

Church looked at him seriously, his earlier humor set aside. "It's necessary to administer electric shocks periodically when they're in captivity; keeps them from going into a dormant state. I have four more adult specimens aboard in semicryogenic kennels. They don't live long isolated from their clan like this. I have to get all I can out of them."

Crespi turned back to the screen, studied the angry drone. The research might be interesting, sure, but how could he stand to work with the monsters that had slaughtered his friends, his lover, had almost killed *him* . . . ? For months, years after the attack, he had been unable to talk about it, the mere mention of the breed leaving him pale and shaking.

And yet—

"To tell you the truth, I wouldn't mind giving that thing a shock or two for auld lang syne myself. I had a run-in with a nest of them once."

Church's gaze was cool, unreadable. "You don't say."

Crespi looked at the creature alone in the pen, hissing softly again, pivoting its obscene head slowly from side to side.

"Yes. Years ago, a long time . . . on a rock near Solano's moon. They attacked my squadron and killed everyone but me. We knew they were dangerous, of course, but we didn't know—" He faltered, searched for the right words, and came up blank. "I didn't know how they *were*."

Crespi couldn't seem to pull his gaze away from the drone. He felt like he was sinking back into the memories of that horrible day, memories he had tried hard to lose. "What I remember—all I remember is that skin, that stink, flashes of teeth. Gibbs, he—"

He looked at Church and realized he was babbling

about things that the doctor probably had already had
experience with.

"Anyway, everyone died."

Church's eyes were still without emotion. "Dear
me, how *awful* for you."

Crespi nodded, tried to regroup. That was a long
time ago, a lifetime. He pushed the memories away,
refocused on Church.

"Say, didn't I read that you survived an encounter
as well?" He had, in Church's stat sheet before he'd
left Earth. Nothing specific except the date, some
forty years ago—

"Sir, the system is ready."

Crespi started, turned. A young tech in a clean gray
coverall had joined them.

Church smiled. "Very good, Hawks." He motioned
at Crespi. "This is Colonel Doctor Crespi, he's here to
uncover our—illegal operation."

Hawks snapped a salute, his face uncertain. "How
do you do, sir. Illegal operation? I don't understand."

Church walked to another vid screen, calling out
over his shoulder. "That's all right, Hawks, neither
does he. Just step over here, Doctor."

Crespi returned the salute impatiently and followed
Church. He wasn't here to swap horror stories. The
shock of seeing a live drone again was wearing off
rapidly; it was time for a few straight answers.

*Is it, Doctor? Or is it just time to avoid remember-
ing anymore?*

Crespi told his mind to shut up.

The screen they stood in front of was bigger and
showed a different view of the pen. Crespi frowned
as a door slid open from the enclosure to some type

of corridor, probably into the labyrinth of sublevel passageways that he had seen on Church's layout grid.

The older man spoke softly, as if explaining to a child. "That door leads into the maze. Once inside, the creature will be confronted with choices. Let's see if you can second-guess its behavior."

Crespi scowled, opened his mouth to speak—and then thought better. The video image changed, the camera angle from behind the drone as it cautiously moved into the corridor. There was a small table, bolted into the wall of the passage—and on top was a pig, a real pig, drugged or asleep. And next to that—

"There's a man in there!" Crespi could hear the anxiety in his own voice. The guy was armored and armed, but *Jesus*, what was Church *doing*?

The bespectacled doctor nodded calmly. "Yes. Aliens don't have eyes, they can't be fooled by holograms. But don't worry, I've taken every precaution. If the alien attacks, the automatic sensors will activate the electrodes.

"Now, Crespi—that drone is starving, and as you may know, these creatures are very fond of pig. What will it do?"

Church was relaxed, self-assured. Obviously he couldn't go around killing volunteers, the project would have to be full-proof safe—although Crespi wondered just what the hell they had offered that man to go in there alone.

He swallowed, tried to consider the question clearly.

"Well. I know it won't retreat, but . . ." *Starving, the*

thing's starving. "I think it'll attack the pig, eat, and then attack the man."

The drone crept closer to the two choices, hissing low in its dark throat.

"Wrong, Crespi." Church's voice was a whisper. "R-O-N-G, wrong."

The alien shrieked and lunged for the suited man, its talons extended. Crespi just had time to see the terror on the poor man's face before he raised his weapon, too late—

A flash of brilliance and the drone screamed again, this time in frustration and pain. It crumpled to the floor, dazed, steam or smoke rising up from its black exoskeleton. The armed man was pale, but unharmed. He backed up to a door a few meters behind him and exited quickly.

Church went on as if nothing particularly interesting had happened. "As you saw, it barely hesitated. It will starve to death before it will neglect an opportunity to attack an enemy."

Crespi nodded, willed his pounding heart to slow down.

Church gestured at the unmoving drone on the screen. "I believe they don't consider themselves as individuals; they fight for their species, not themselves. They cannot be frightened, intimidated, or bribed into not attacking, as a threat to one is a threat to all—and to leave that threat standing is to go against their basic instinctual drive. Pain, fatigue, overwhelming odds . . . nothing mitigates their aggression.

He nodded toward the vid. The drone had pulled itself to its feet slowly and now hissed at its unseen enemy.

Church smiled faintly. "As you can see, it's up and at 'em again. And in a minute, it will have to make another choice."

The alien moved closer to the pig, and the cameras switched to an overhead view. Crespi could see that there was a chain binding one of the pig's legs to the table. The noise of the attack had woken it somewhat, and it grunted sleepily as the creature approached.

To the left of the food animal was a small passage set into the floor. The alien stood between the pig and the exit way, its tail clattering lightly on the floor behind it.

Church enlarged the vid slightly with the touch of a button. "Here it is confronted with a choice between food and the possibility of escape. That small tunnel leads to a storage room. The alien can sense that there are no men down the tunnel; if it wants to escape, that's the route to take."

Crespi raised his eyebrows. The drone would want the food, but against the chance to escape . . . ?

The creature turned toward the passageway as the pig whuffled to itself. Crespi felt his muscles relax slightly; he hadn't even realized how tense he had been until—

The drone spun, shrieked, and tore the now-screaming pig off of the chain. The high-pitched squeals of the terrified animal filled the lab as the monstrous black talons pierced its hide, spewing thick streams of blood against the walls.

The alien thrust its head forward and its inner jaws shot out and tore into the flesh of the helpless pig. The animal seemed to explode into a mass of writhing, dying flesh, the heavy blood spraying the drone's malefic form as it shrieked again in conquest.

No electrodes this time. Crespi turned away from the screen, unable to watch the creature feed. And as he turned, he saw Church studying the video image intently.

Church was smiling.

8

McGuinness finally leaned back from the com in her sparse quarters and willed herself to relax. She'd spent over an hour hooked into the station's main system, but the accessible stuff wasn't going to tell her what she needed—although truthfully, she wasn't even sure exactly what that was. Names and numbers that probably weren't even attainable unless one had a code slate for them. She could probably rascal it out given time, *if* she knew where to look. Or what to look for.

She sighed, staring at the blank screen of the outmoded personal in front of her. She'd *trained* on a piece better than this, and that had been—

Fifteen *years* ago? Christ on a crutch. If someone had told her then where she'd be now, she would've laughed until she cried. Or maybe just cried. A class-three systems tech who *could* be making a hundred-fifty creds an hour writing forensics programs—still in the Corps, stuck on some backward science station digging for secrets.

She chewed at her lower lip thoughtfully. She was no spy; she shouldn't even have come, let alone reenlisted. She could have been out six months ago, free and clear.

Except if I don't do it, who will?

Right. Nobody would, and she would have gone on with her life, maybe the only person who could uncover the truth about whatever the hell was going on here. And every day would bring fresh pain, the knowledge that she had sold her memories . . .

She shook her head, not wanting to think about it; she was here to find out what Doctor Church was hiding, and would have to try to keep her emotions out of it. Church or maybe Thaves would fuck up, or maybe it would be something as simple as a misplaced document or some contraband chemical trace; she'd need to be on her toes, prepared. Between hacking and her forensics background, something would turn up.

Until then, she would have to wait. Patience wasn't one of her strong suits, but she needed evidence before she could approach Crespi. And until something out of the ordinary occurred, she wouldn't know where to start.

She sighed again, stood up. Orientation was still an hour plus away, where she'd be assigned station duties and set to work. Maybe she could duck into the noncom lounge and ask a few questions—

The com bleated and a few lines of data appeared on the screen. McGuinness leaned over, frowned.

//All authorized TFC and systems monitors report to stations immediately/Security breach K4 Class 07//

She felt her gut tighten. Technically, she wasn't authorized to do anything, yet—but if she just happened to wander over to one of the console stations, oblivious to the alert . . .

McGuinness grabbed her temp ID and headed for the door. It was probably too much to hope for, this soon, but this could be the key to it all—the event that would lead to some peace for her troubled mind, and to the eventual ruin of Paul Church.

Church let the drone devour about half of the slaughtered pig before reluctantly shocking it once again into submission; he liked to watch them eat, the veracity of it, the unadulterated pleasure they took in their conquests . . .

Two heavily armed techs crept into the passage and cleared away the rest of the dripping carcass, never taking their eyes off of the fallen creature.

"Can't let it eat too much," he said. "If it gorges in its weakened condition, it may die."

Crespi seemed interested, but he still had that stubborn set to his jaw, the petulant look of a little boy who was determined not to give in.

Well, that will change soon enough.

"I'm sure you noticed that it didn't just kill that pig, it practically swam into it. Fearful prey seems to attract aliens and stimulate them to make especially messy kills; I don't think it's a form of play, exactly, but they do seem to enjoy it."

Crespi swallowed, hard, then nodded. He seemed

uncomfortable, which was disappointing; obviously his emotional state was influencing his scientific mind, a problem that Church had successfully conquered decades before. It could be hard to overcome, but a true scholar would find a way in their search for the greater truth. At least he was paying attention, that was a start ...

Two different techs entered the labyrinth and waited for the alien to stir. One held an automatic machine rifle while the other stood unarmed.

The drone hissed softly and stumbled to its feet, turning its long head slowly, back and forth.

Church tried again to involve Crespi in the game. "Care to guess which one it'll attack?"

Crespi hesitated, then cleared his throat. "Uh—the armed man?"

Even as he spoke, the drone lunged for the man with the rifle, quickly and silently. The naked terror on the man's face was almost comical; the sensors kicked in, as always, dropping the haggard creature to the floor in an electric pulse of energy.

Church was pleased. "Good call, Doctor! An alien will always attack a perceived threat. Out of the hundreds of similar tests I've run on dozens of aliens, there has never been a single deviation from this rule."

Crespi looked at him, seemingly irritated. "Hundreds of tests? Dozens—what you're telling me is tantamount to a confession, Church."

Church sighed inwardly, stared blandly back at him. Couldn't he see what was in front of him? This was the type of research that men like him would *kill* to get into, and here he was playing soldier boy for a group of paranoid brass. It was pathetic, really, that he should limit himself so—and more than a little annoying.

Crespi held his gaze for a moment, then frowned and looked away. "Okay, let's overlook that for the time being. You've determined some extremely simple behavior patterns—so what's the point of all this repeat experimentation?"

Finally!

"It's not repetitious. Each time the maze is set up, new sensory equipment is built into it. I'm compiling a data overview that will set a new standard of bioanalysis."

Church glanced at the screen, saw Copper and that other one, Wagner, step into the alien's corridor. The creature was just beginning to move.

"Now you'll see something interesting," he said softly. "Neither man is armed, but the one in the back is full of FITR, a telepathine that induces a sense of invulnerability and increased mental strength."

Truly, Copper looked like he was ready to eat the fallen creature; his head was up, his shoulders back, and he wore a slight snarl, as if daring the alien to make a move.

"The other man is cold sober and, as you can see, scared half out of his mind. Watch."

Again, the drone pulled itself up from the floor, moved toward the two men. It barely paused before leaping for Wagner, who screamed, held up one hand as if to ward off the attack.

And this time, the sensor didn't go off.

Crespi watched as the drone leapt, and—
ohshit

—where was the electric shock? The creature was almost on top of the sober and terrified lab tech, about to rip him to shreds!

The drugged man stepped forward, stared at the moving drone as if he meant to kill it with a look. The shrieking alien reached out, talons spread—

And faltered. Stopped cold in its tracks.

Only then did the flash of electric pulse fill the video screen, jolting the drone to collapse.

Church was excited, practically jumping up and down. "There, did you see that?!"

Crespi looked away from the screen, where the two men were being led out by two others. The tech that the alien had almost killed was shaking uncontrollably.

"I'm not sure *what* I saw. It started to attack but then—it seemed to change its mind."

"Not quite. First it went for the scared man; what caused it to pause was the will of the drugged man." Church began to pace, hands behind his back.

"Aliens communicate with each other telepathically. They can sense fear in other animals. My working hypothesis is that they can physically 'see' the minds of men, but cannot understand them."

Crespi shrugged. "I suppose that's plausible, but—"

"But what? You just saw that alien waver during an attack. Have you ever heard of such a thing before? The man under the influence of FITR was *willing* the drone to stop its attack, and it did!"

Church had stopped in front of him and Crespi could suddenly see something that he had somehow missed before. There was a light in the older doctor's eyes, a glittering sheen that radiated intelligence and inspiration. A light of genius.

Or madness . . .

"Doctor Crespi. This and previous experiments indicate that a weakened alien can have its actions influenced by a human mind in an exalted state."

Church paused, perhaps to let that sink in. Crespi suddenly felt far less objective than he'd wanted. God, was it possible?

"If what you're saying is true," he began, then hesitated. "The implications—"

Church grinned. "If it's true, I'll prove it. This research has just begun. Think of it, Crespi—synthetic E waves! Aliens reduced to fawning puppies at the touch of a button! Entire hives turned into petting zoos!"

The grin dropped a few notches, and Church turned that bland stare toward him again. "But a bit too esoteric for traditional venues of research, eh? Risky, messy, inconclusive—possibly even immoral. Profound potential for misuse . . . a pearl beyond price. Secrets countermanding secrets, official smokescreens—"

Church innocently looked away. "—even top investigative men sent to see how much can be found out."

Crespi scowled. "What are you saying?"

Church ignored the question, returned it with another. "Why don't we have you coded into the bioscan now?"

Crespi paused, uncertain. He had been taken for some ride already, but the offer was made: he was welcome to join the research. Just watching the creature had been hard enough, but to be involved—? Could he do it?

The ashen, beautiful face of Cady Trask suddenly welled up into his mind, as she had been before disappearing into the darkness forever, mutilated and then killed by the obscene nest of monsters. The scent of melting rock, the smoke in his eyes; the weeks after his recovery spent with the psych module; the night terrors and the hopeless self-hatred that had taken years to overcome, the final truth that he had been unable to do any more than he *had* done . . .

Could he do it?

How could he not?

This was big, really big, something that could finally make a difference. Church was a strange one, but the work was innovative, exciting—and potentially lethal for the alien breed. Admiral Pickman could be sent a vague report on something connected, maybe about telepathy work—not a lie, exactly . . .

But God, the dangers involved! How up front had Church been with him, how far was he willing to go with this?

One question, and he would accept.

"How many crew members have died during the course of your research?"

Church smiled, eyes still shining with that inner light.

"It depends on who you ask." That odd humor, almost taunting.

"I'm asking you."

Church didn't pause, met his gaze squarely. "None."

Crespi studied his face for a moment, the deeply etched lines around his sharp gaze. He nodded slowly.

"It would be a pleasure to work with you, Doctor."

Church smiled widely and nodded in return. "Good."

A young woman hurried over to them, her boot

heels clacking loudly against the polished floor. Her expression was worried, her brow heavy.

"Excuse me, Colonel Doctor Church—was the specimen in K4 transferred?" Her voice seemed tremulous, uncertain.

Church answered slowly. "Transferred? No."

The woman, a forensics tech by the uniform, bit her lip, apparently deeply anxious. "Something's wrong then, sir." She took a deep breath, swallowed.

"The door to Kennel 4 is open—and the alien is gone."

9

Church didn't skip a beat.

"You're sure?"

The woman nodded. "Yes, we've looked—"

But Church was already striding away, calling out orders as he moved. Crespi followed, as confused as he had been all day; it wasn't *possible*, not with the supposedly escape-proof pens, the monitoring systems—

Unless somebody let it out.

The thought chilled him.

"—out the alert immediately. Williams, secure the floor, then get to the trackers. Briggs, inform Admiral Thaves, and, uh"— Church looked around quickly— "Webster, get me a head count."

A chorus of "yessirs" as Church hurried up the steps to the viewing deck and back toward the guarded entry. Crespi hurried to catch up as the aging doctor barked orders at the sentries.

"Secure this door. Get reinforcements and cover the lab perimeter!"

"Yes, sir!"

Church was moving at a half run now, and Crespi jogged along behind him, through a maze of turns and twists to what he assumed would be the monitoring center. He couldn't help the fear, that they would turn a corner and there it would be, long and black and shrieking for blood . . .

He shook the thought and picked up his pace. This was a day for the books all right, un-fuckin'-believable. It was all happening too fast, the memories stirred by that drone, the drone itself, the bizarre twist that he suddenly *wanted* to be here, doing this—

No, not this, research is one thing—hunting down killing machines isn't what I want, never again—

Church was talking, trying to explain. "—impossible, but we've prepared for the impossible; the aliens are all wearing tracking devices, so it's just a matter of time . . ."

He trailed off as they turned down one more corridor and entered one of the rooms. The walls were covered with dozens of small vid units, watched closely by several worried techs.

Crespi saw Sharon McGuinness standing behind one of the seated men, her knuckles white against the back of his chair. She looked up tensely as the two men hurried into the room.

"Situation!" Church called out.

A voice blared out from one of the intercom systems. "Colonel Doctor Church, all personnel are accounted for except Lieutenant Mortenson."

Church stepped over to a grid monitor. "Get Mortenson on camera! I'll find the alien."

Crespi ran a hand through his hair and looked around helplessly. There was nothing for him to do except watch and wait. McGuinness seemed to be in the same boat, and he caught her gaze for a moment, saw the frustration there before they both turned back to the screens.

"What's the status?" A booming voice filled the room as Admiral Thaves stormed in, his face red.

Church held up one hand, effectively silencing him and reaffirming Crespi's suspicions: Church was in charge here, rank aside.

Church pointed at three red dots on the grided screen. "There are the kenneled ones . . ." He glanced down as the vid monitor beneath lit up. "And there's Mortenson. What the devil is he doing?"

Crespi peered over Church's shoulder. A thin, middle-aged man in a work uniform knelt amid a pile of decontamination suits. As the audio became clear, Crespi could tell that the man was humming.

Church went back to the upper screen, talking softly to himself as the station's prints flickered by rapidly. "Oh, where, oh, where has my little dog— *there*, freeze it!" He jabbed one finger at the small red dot. "In that breaker room!"

Right next to Mortenson.

The tech seated to Church's left spoke quickly. "Shall I put Mortenson on com, sir?"

Church shook his head. "Let me do it. That alien is only twenty yards away, if that. If Mortenson panics, it'll be over in a millisecond."

Church reached over and tapped a button. "Mortenson, this is Colonel Doctor Church."

The man's reaction would have been funny if not for the circumstances. He jerked to his feet and looked around wildly, shocked by the voice from nowhere, dropping the tool he'd held.

"Uh, yessir! Colonel Doctor Church, sir." He regained his composure, looked up at the nearest camera.

Church spoke calmly, firmly. "I want you to go directly to the compressor room in SJ 12."

Confusion played across Mortenson's thin features. "Right away, sir?"

"Yes, immediately. I want you there in six seconds."

Behind Crespi, Thaves muttered angrily. "What is that nitwit doing futzing around with those suits?"

The vid image switched, showed Mortenson as he walked quickly down a shadowy corridor. He was on one of the lower levels of the station, primarily a maintenance and storage area. Mortenson hurried, but didn't seem frightened.

Crespi felt his heart pounding with each of the tech's steps. God, if he had any *idea* . . .

Mortenson walked into the compressor room and addressed the camera there, set at eye level just inside the door. "I'm here, sir. Do you copy?"

Church cracked a tight grin. "Big and bold, Mortenson. Shut the door behind you and lock it, please."

Mortenson glanced away for a second and then back to the camera. The audio clearly picked up the sound of the door sliding firmly shut.

Crespi could feel the combined tension in the monitor room give way. He exhaled heavily, not realizing until then that he had been holding his breath.

"Yes, sir. Anything else?"

Church rolled his head back. "Yes. Give thanks. You just had a close squeak."

Mortenson frowned. "What's the problem, sir?"

The admiral stepped forward and shouted at the video image.

"This is Admiral Thaves. What the *hell* were you doing with those decon suits?"

Mortenson shrank back from the com and spoke nervously. "I was changing the filters, sir."

"On whose authority?"

"Station's orders, sir. Is there a problem?"

Crespi had looked away, almost embarrassed by Thaves's blustering reaction to the crisis. What he saw made him spin back to the screen, terrified.

A moving red dot.

Before he could speak, he saw it. They all saw it, suddenly dropping into the video image directly behind the unknowing Mortenson.

"God," Crespi whispered.

The escaped drone hung upside down, perhaps supported by some unseen pipe overhead. First its shiny long head, the dripping teeth—and the spindly black arm as it reached—

Church screamed first, the others in the room echoing the words. "Mortenson, get out of there!"

Still, he didn't know. The thin-faced man held up his hands in apology, addressed the com. "But, sir, I was just—"

He didn't finish the sentence, *couldn't* finish, as those sharp talons wrapped around his throat and lifted him, as easily as a man lifts a feather.

He let out a strangled cry, not knowing what had him, what pulled him closer to the extending jaws—

His choked scream cut off as the rod of the alien's

inner teeth shot forward, into and through the back of his skull. It gave as easily as wet tissue and the image was suddenly blasted red, his blood on the lens.

Then there was only red, and the vaguest image of movement behind the crimson veil. Sickening wet noises, the sound of gristle being chewing blaring out into the stunned room.

Church reached over and shut off the audio. He looked away from the muted redness and spoke softly. "Hawkins, you and Stockdale suit up and subdue that creature."

Thaves spoke angrily, but his face was pale. "What was that man doing down there in the first place? Station's orders, my ass."

Church glanced at him. "Sir, if I may respectfully submit—whatever he was doing there is now a matter of secondary importance."

Crespi wanted to be sick. Church's voice was calm, only the slightest undertone of tension. The muted, bleary picture was one of gnashing teeth and thick, bloody wetness.

Thaves turned toward the door, seeming to regain some of his bluster. "Church, I expect the results of a comprehensive investigation in my hands by 0800 tomorrow."

"Yes, sir," Church said quietly. He turned back to the screen, expressionless, watched the obscured movements for a moment.

Finally, he sighed, pointed at one of the suited technicians. "Blackman, you and . . ."

McGuinness had moved to join them. Church looked at her. "Who are you?"

"Sharon McGuinness, sir. TFC."

Church cocked an eyebrow at her, and something

like recognition flashed through his gaze. "McGuinness ..."

Whatever it was, it was gone. Church cleared his
throat and went on. "Blackman, you and McGuinness
confirm that the alien has been reconfined. And then
I want you to cordon off sector SJ and begin a surface
analysis."

He looked down at the tech who was seated in
front of the monitor, a burly, dark-skinned man. "Williams, clean and close the lab. I want live guards at
the kennel."

"Yes, sir."

Church stood for a moment, seemingly lost in
thought, one hand against his chin. His shoulders
were slumped, his face drawn. Crespi felt some sympathy for him; the doctor had done all he'd been able
to do, and it wasn't enough.

And you know what that feels like, don't you?

Church glanced up at Crespi. "I'll meet you in the
lab in eight hours." He seemed about to say more, but
then turned and slowly walked away. He looked—
beaten, a man who'd lost everything.

"Certainly. I'll be in my quarters," said Crespi, and
Church waved halfheartedly over one shoulder in response before exiting.

Crespi stood there, feeling depressed and worn
out. He glanced at his watch and sighed. Barely two
hours into his new assignment, and more had happened already than had occurred in the last two *years*
of his work on Earth.

Suddenly he felt certain that he shouldn't have
come, that he was foolish to have taken an assignment he'd known nothing about. He felt almost nostalgic for that vague anxiety he'd had that morning on

the transport ship, because at least he hadn't been *here*, on board this station. There was something wrong here, something deadly wrong—

Ease up, Crespi, things will work out. You're just having a bad day—

No. Lieutenant *Mortenson* had had a bad day; he was just in a very dark and shitty mood, and what he needed was to go sit down somewhere and try to relax.

Crespi sighed again and went to find his quarters.

McGuinness hurried down the dingy corridor, her heart pounding. She mentally called out the numbers of each door she passed, praying that Crespi would be home.

85—87—*there*, A89. She stopped in front of his quarters, took a deep breath. She'd have to take it slow, no blurting out accusations that she couldn't back up; what she *knew*, deep down, and what she could prove were still separate things . . .

Another deep breath, and she punched the buzzer. After a brief pause, Crespi's voice floated out over the com.

"Yes?"

"It's Lieutenant McGuinness, sir."

"Come in, McGuinness."

Crespi sat to the side of a small, faded couch against the wall of his room. She glanced around briefly; officer's quarters were bigger, a few extra chairs, but nothing to write home about—

"May I sit down, sir?"

Crespi nodded, gesturing vaguely to the couch, his

face pale; Mortenson's death was only a few hours old.

"I thought you'd still be at the accident site."

McGuinness sat down next to him, pushed her hair back behind her ears. "We did some prelim and spec-ification, and now the sweeps are down there."

Crespi's gaze sharpened, perhaps at the tension in her voice. "Find anything?"

She spoke calmly and clearly. "The tracking device on the escaped alien had been partially cut off. Cut, as with a blade. We found it in the breaker room; no alien residue."

Crespi stared at her, then lowered his head into his hands. "Oh, boy."

McGuinness went on. "In the generator room we found a substance smeared on the pipes where the alien was hiding. Smelled like pheromone."

Crespi kept his head down. "I don't think I want to hear this," he mumbled.

"It gets worse. Mortenson *was* there on station's or-ders."

There.

Crespi looked up, frowned. She met his gaze.

"The kennel door was opened by the station, too."

"You're saying that was a deliberate killing—?"

"It sure looks that way, Sir."

She waited, watched his incredulity turn, could al-most see a sharp decisiveness come into his eyes. And then he asked the question that she had most hoped for, had desperately wanted to be asked.

"Can you unscramble the station code and trace that order on the mainline?"

She paused, not wanting to seem too eager. This was the tricky part, and she hoped that Crespi would bite; without him, she was strictly on her own. "Not without authorization . . ."

He nodded, made the decision without blinking. "You have it. Sub rosa, McGuinness, and don't get caught. Report only to me. Do you understand?"

"Yes, sir."

"I want this to be our little secret," he said, and smiled briefly. Dismissively.

She stood and walked out, waiting until the door closed before she let her own smile surface.

The trap was set.

Church would never know what hit him.

Paul Church steepled his fingers against his chin and nodded slowly, watching as Crespi brought his meeting to an end.

"I want this to be our little secret," he said, his low voice somewhat muffled-sounding as it crackled out over the video's com. The microphone needed to be replaced; Church would have to see to that.

Church leaned back in his office chair as McGuinness left Crespi's room, still nodding. He'd figured on something like this from the good doctor—in fact, he would've been surprised if Crespi or one of his underlings *hadn't* done a bit of digging. The question was, how to use it? It was moot at this point, not enough had happened to worry about trump cards . . . but all information was useful, and he filed it away under things to remember.

A secret, to be sure; Church wouldn't tell a soul.

10

Church closed his eyes and remembered.

So many secrets . . .

There had been nine on board when they'd set down, ten if he included Judith—and he had to include her, synth or no. He'd lost his virginity to Judith, and had loved her deeply, if blindly, since he'd been about twelve. She was there primarily to keep the small crew sexually satisfied, but had also been programmed as a botanist; she tended the small garden on board the *Incunabulum*, their ship, and usually prepared their meals.

Jason and Lucian Church, his parents. The crew, three men: Taylor, Hewett, and Johanson. They did most of the heavy work. And for that last, happy month, three more—Quentin and Louise Clark, both scientists, and their daughter, Rebecca. Rebecca had been beautiful, perhaps even more beautiful than Judith, who could never change, never grow older—never return Paul's infatuation. Rebecca was only two years older than Paul, and seemed *almost* as interested in him as he was in her; almost was close enough for him to dream about her . . .

So there had been ten of them, on their blissfully ignorant way to RLW 1289, a large settlement on a recently colonized planet where they would drop off the Clarks and then continue onward. Church's parents were terraformers, "doing God's work," they used to say, then laugh, gazing at their young son and each other with fondness and affection.

Only one stop before RLW 1289, a routine data pickup, a time box from a small moon that had been terraformed fifteen years before. Paul had looked forward to the stop, had hoped that perhaps he and Rebecca could slip away, walk together through the man-made Eden and share some of their secrets with each other. Paul wanted to be a scientist, had even gotten a small grant from the government at the age of nineteen, for immunization research. His parents had been so proud! And he so full of youth, of ideals and questions and the desire to be loved . . .

And God help them, they'd set down.

Lucian Church couldn't seem to stop frowning. "Do you think it's safe?"

Paul's father shrugged easily, but he sounded a bit tense. "I'm sure it's nothing. And if they're not supposed to be there, we can lift off again, okay?" He smiled reassuringly at her before turning back to the controls.

"Everybody hold on, we're going in."

The *Incunabulum* swept down through the clear and set down near the Genesis station, only a few hundred meters from the strange ship. Jason Church was a superlative pilot, only the barest jolt as the landers touched the ground.

Paul and the others unbuckled their harnesses, stood, and stretched. Rebecca smiled nervously at Paul and he returned it, trying to look calmer than he felt. Terraformed worlds were off-limits to general travel, and he shared his parents' concern; there wasn't supposed to be anyone here, and yet the sensors had picked up a ship—a ship that hadn't responded to their hail.

Paul heard Rebecca's mother whisper anxiously to her husband. "Smugglers?"

The scientist shook his head. "I don't know, love. I hope not."

Paul's father walked to the door and then smiled tightly at them. "Judith, why don't you and I go see what there is to see? The rest of you, just hold tight, we'll be right back—"

Lucian Church frowned again, but nodded, and Paul felt somewhat relieved; Judith was as strong as any of the three crewmen but with better reflexes, designed not to let any bodily harm come to her human shipmates. If any harm was to be had.

The two left the ship, the door sealing behind them. Paul and the others crowded up to the console to watch on the small viewing screen.

It was hard to imagine anything bad happening in such a beautiful place. Paul had seen over a dozen planets and moons just like it, but each time he was struck by the sight—a new world, untainted by humanity. The Genesis programs were truly amazing, and his parents were good at what they did—each project created an untamed wilderness, green and bursting with life.

Judith and Paul's father reached the strange ship, a basic low-grade class-nine jumper. The ramp was down, and Judith went in first; after a moment, Jason followed.

After only a few seconds, they reappeared, Paul's father making exaggerated shrugging motions toward the *Incunabulum*. The group sighed collectively, and Paul felt Rebecca's hand catch his own and squeeze it lightly before letting it go. He felt a sudden flush of warmth for her, as well as a slight stirring in his groin.

Jesus, Paul, grow up! He grinned at her and hoped he wasn't blushing. Almost twenty-one and responding like a *virgin*. True, she was the first girl he'd really spent any time with since puberty (well, not including Judith), but *still* . . .

His father was waving for them to come down, and Paul felt his heart leap in his chest; he loved their life, their travels and all that, but to set his feet on the ground again—there was nothing like it, nothing at all. They usually stopped for an hour or two, spent some time just lounging around outside, breathing *real* air, the only human beings on an entire world—

Well, maybe not this time. Where were the pilots of the other ship? Weird.

Josh Hewett, the oldest of the three crewmen, broke out their small weapons cache and distributed the half-dozen stun-wands among them. Paul tucked his in one of his vest pockets, vaguely excited at the prospect of trouble. There wouldn't be any, of course, there never was, so he allowed himself the fantasy of taking out bad guys, saving Rebecca from a fate worse than death—

"Sweetheart, are you coming?" His mother stood at the door, smiling gently at her son. God, she was actually *beaming*, and Rebecca was watching, a smug little smile on her own dark, pretty face. That smile was too much, it just screamed, *aw, isn't that cute.*

Sheeit. Paul nodded, tried to look like the scientist he was in spite of the fact that he suddenly felt about nine years old.

"Uh, yeah, I just wanted to grab some juice. I'll be right down."

His mother nodded, then walked down the ramp, Rebecca behind her. Paul rolled his eyes, then went to the cooler.

Just him left on board, except for Taylor. The crewman was digging through his pack, probably looking for one of his stinky cigars. He smirked over at Paul.

"Got a little girlfriend, Paul?"

Paul scowled. "Shut up, dickhead. At least I wouldn't have to *share*."

Taylor smiled innocently. "Hey, Judy don't mind. And who says Rebecca wouldn't share? Who says she hasn't already?"

Paul tried to look angry, but he couldn't pull it off. He laughed, and after a second Taylor joined in.

Paul grabbed a juice bulb and walked out onto the ramp. It was a gorgeous day, perhaps midafternoon on this one's cycle. The air was cool and crisp, with just the faintest undertone of—

Paul frowned, sniffed. Decay? That was unusual after only fifteen years—maybe a storm had killed something recently, though it didn't smell like plant matter exactly . . .

"Hey, you want to move or do I knock you off?"

Taylor stood behind him, an unlit cigar in his grinning teeth.

"Yeah, sure," he mumbled, then hurried down the ramp, suddenly not in the mood for banter and not certain why. He walked quickly to meet the others, who stood gathered near the station, by the box holder.

He'd read about Eden in the history modules, the garden that the original man and woman had supposedly been ejected from—and surely the writers had imagined a place as beautiful as this as they had penned those words. Lush with bounty, as pure and fresh as a new thought—it was the stuff of waking dreams, those light, sweet fantasies just before consciousness reared. It *was* Eden, or as close as humanity could ever come—

Beware the serpent . . .

Paul grinned at his own pessimism; a downside to every perfection, of course.

His father had entered the code for the release and was chatting with the Clarks when Paul caught up.

"—not a clue. Looks like the ship's been deserted for at least a couple of years, by the dust. Plenty of supplies, too."

Louise Clark had her arms crossed tightly. She looked nervous.

"Maybe some sort of sickness, the crew got sick and died here. Do you smell something? I noticed it when we got off, like mold of some kind, organic. But perhaps—human?"

"I noticed it, too," said Paul. "It *does* seem different."

Jason Church removed the slim box from the holder and then nodded. "All right. We've got what we came for—we'd better just leave, contact the Company when we get back in range, and tell them about it; it's not our job to check this out."

He smiled at Paul and then raised his voice for the others to hear. "No picnic today, folks! Sorry!"

A few good-natured groans from the scattered crewmen, but Paul felt something in his chest loosen: good. That ship and that weird odor had put a damper on things. He and Rebecca would just have to—

He heard something then that froze his thoughts, froze everyone around him into tense silence.

Chittering. An animal sound, definitely not human—and like no animal he'd ever heard.

But there aren't any animals—

Now a sound like metal on metal, but not mechanical. Alive.

"What the—" Taylor, behind him.

A flash of movement from behind the Genesis station, dark and incredibly fast. First one, then another—then a dozen, darting into view faster than his stunned mind could count.

Rebecca screamed, pointed, but they could all see.

Alien drones. Paul had heard of them, they all had.

Johanson pulled his wand, but it would be useless if the stories held any merit whatsoever.

Paul spun, looked back at the ship, suddenly too far away. Three or four of the dark, twisted shapes capered and crouched around it.

He turned back, this time as Quentin Clark screamed out his wife's name. One of the impossibly formed creatures had dropped down, grabbed Louise Clark, and held her pinned with its spiny arms.

Paul heard the blast of a stun-wand, then another, and only the angry, high-pitched squeals of the unharmed drones in response.

As if on cue, the aliens shrieked en masse and leapt forward to take the others, their horrible, ridged tails whipping behind them.

Paul cried out, turned to run—

—and dark, cold arms snared him, forced his struggling limbs to his sides.

They were doomed, all of them, only brutal, terrifying death to come, their bodies ripped to bloody pieces by the alien monsters . . .

Church opened his eyes.

If only we had been so fortunate.

11

They had cleaned up Mortenson as best they could, but even the plastiskin patch that covered most of his face couldn't hide the brutal truth—that the lower half of the man's head was gone, and (Crespi thought uneasily) resting in the bowels of a kenneled drone.

Well, at least the bag is mostly zipped.

Mortenson's corpse lay on a gurney in front of the small assembled group, the body bag fastened all the way up to a technician's facsimile of his nose. Not many had chosen to attend the funeral, and Crespi was starting to wish that he'd opted out as well; even patched up, the lieutenant was a mess.

Crespi was exhausted already, and it was only 0900; he had slept for shit the night before, even though he'd turned in reasonably early. Church had buzzed him shortly after McGuinness had left his quarters and canceled their meeting in the lab, saying that the investigation report for Thaves was going to keep him up late. Crespi had choked down dinner and gone to bed, where he'd been haunted by Mortenson's dying face all night long, the dreams tinted a wet shade of crimson.

If Church had been up late, it didn't show. He stood next to the gurney, his head bowed, but his shoulders were straight and his eyes clear.

McGuinness walked in and joined the few other technicians grouped loosely around the room. If any of them had been close to Mortenson, he couldn't tell. The atmosphere in the chill storage bay was subdued, but there were no tears, no expressions of sadness.

Apparently the station had no spiritual adviser, and Crespi didn't think the admiral would want to speak, so he wasn't particularly surprised when Church cleared his throat and began.

"I, uh, can't say that I knew Lieutenant Mortenson well, and in all honesty, that I really wanted to. I think anyone would agree that we were very unlike one another."

Church reached down, placed one hand against the dead man's waxen forehead. "It's been said that there is more difference between two men than between two animals of different species. I believe that, but I feel that Mortenson and I shared something that made us brothers—our humanity."

Church moved his hand down to the bag's zipper and pulled up, the sound of the plastic teeth loud in the silent room. "If we had ever compared our life stories," he continued, "I'm sure that we would have found much in common. We each experienced the strange ignorance of childhood, the difficulties of young manhood, the sacred achings that came with first love—"

Church looked down at the covered corpse somberly. "Now everything that was a man in him is at an end. No more satisfaction, no more joy—but also no more frustration . . . or fear.

"We consign his remains to the void. There is nothing more to be said, except—good-bye."

Somebody coughed. Church bowed his head again for a few seconds and then looked over at one of the two medical noncoms who stood nearby.

"Take the body to the discharge bay."

Crespi frowned. Not much of a farewell. Already the small crowd was dispersing.

God, I hope I get better than that.

Admiral Thaves stepped forward, held up one hand. "Just a minute. Colonel Doctor Church, Mortenson signed an organ donor release. You might want to keep the body—"

Church shook his head. "That's unnecessary, Admiral. Protocol dictates that any man killed—"

Thaves cut him off, pointing one meaty finger at Church. "Don't you dare recite the damn rule book to me!"

Church didn't flinch. "I beg your pardon, sir."

Crespi watched, curious to see if Thaves would back down, although he already knew the answer.

Not if, but how.

The admiral scowled for a moment, then waved his hand dismissively. "It's your call, Church. I just thought the dumb, dead bastard might be of some use; God knows it's about time he was."

Church spoke softly. "I respectfully submit that burial in space with military honors is appropriate."

Thaves was already walking away, grumbling under his breath. "Fine, fine, shoot his ass full of diamonds while you're at it ..."

Church turned back to the medicals and nodded. "Bring him to the discharge tube. I'll jettison him myself."

"Yes, sir."

Church turned, caught sight of Crespi, and nodded. "Nice of you to attend, Doctor."

Crespi stood uncomfortably, not sure of what to say. "It seemed appropriate."

Church watched him, as if waiting for something else.

"Well," he said. "That was quite a speech."

"Oh, you think so?" Church smiled, just the barest quiver at the corners of his mouth—and yet his eyes were bright, full of mirth. He looked as if he were laughing inside, which made Crespi feel even more uncomfortable.

Well, death often inspired some strange reactions. Crespi smiled back tiredly, trying to put the older man at ease. Church was probably dealing with a lot of guilt, and he surely hadn't slept well either ...

Church glanced at his watch. "It will be a few hours before we can meet up at the lab, get back to work. Why don't you go have yourself some R and R?"

"Thanks. I wanted to try out the gym, actually. Why don't you buzz me when you're ready?"

"Fine."

Crespi was walking out of the bay when McGuinness caught up to him.

"Colonel Doctor Crespi, before you go, I wonder if

I could have a word with you ... about new assign-
ments?"

Crespi nodded. *My, how subtle.* "Certainly,
McGuinness."

As they walked out together, Crespi looked back to
see Church smiling after the two of them, eyes still
shining. Terrific; he probably figured they were going
off to get laid, nice impression. Not that McGuinness
wasn't bright and attractive, she was, but—

*Quite attractive, actually; sure you want to hit the
gym ... ?*

Crespi smiled to himself as they walked down the
corridor, heading back up to main levels, but it faded
quickly. A man had died, and someone on board the
Innominata knew why; he needed McGuinness to
find out who it was, and that was all.

Right.

McGuinness led Crespi into the station's main mess
hall, which was mostly deserted at this hour. Perhaps
a dozen or so people milled around, techs and grunts
for the most part, the air thick with the scents of
processed foods and instant coffee.

She motioned toward the viewing window against
the far wall, at the endless night outside.

"We can talk in private over there," she said softly.

Crespi nodded curtly and followed.

In spite of her resolve, her palms were damp and
her heart thumped heavily in her chest. The shit she'd
dug up was deep indeed, and Crespi needed to know
it ASAP—

But he needs to know the rest, too.

She sighed and looked out the window, suddenly

reluctant to share the secret she'd kept for so long. This was her life now, her only life, and the only therapy that she had—the thing that had gotten her moving when she'd been in too much pain to move for herself.

When she'd signed up to come to the station, she'd known that eventually it would have to come out—and probably to Crespi, since he was the one chosen to dig into the *Innominata*'s shadows by the Corps. She trusted his integrity as an officer, but her own reasons probably had very little to do with his . . . and he could decide to turn her out of the loop based on the differences.

Crespi waited.

She took a deep breath, tried to meet his gaze, and found that she couldn't.

"I've found out some disturbing things, sir, but before I tell you, I have to come clean."

Crespi frowned, kept his voice low. "Go on."

"On the transport ship, you asked why I volunteered for this assignment. I didn't tell you, but there *was* a reason. The man you were sent here to replace, David Lennox, he was my . . . fiancé, I guess you could say."

She kept her gaze on the floor now, not wanting to see Crespi's face. "We met five years ago, two years before he was sent here, to be Church's research assistant. He tried repeatedly to have himself transferred, but could never get the orders . . ."

She trailed off, then untabbed her shoulder pocket and took out the still photo that she carried, of her and David years before. She handed it over to Crespi, knowing what he'd see there—a handsome young officer, grinning a goofy grin, his arm around a much happier Sharon McGuinness. There were no lines of pain or sorrow on the girl's face, no shadow in the eyes that she looked at now in the mirror and hardly recognized as her own.

Crespi studied the picture, his features tightening into a scowl.

She hurried on. "He tried to send me a coded message, but it arrived scrambled. Then I was told that he had died of a heart attack—here, on this station. Shortly after, my apartment was burglarized and everything he'd ever sent to me was taken, even—"

She faltered, but went on. "—even love letters. I want—no, I *need* to know what happened here. I *need* to."

It was out, all of it, and in spite of the pain it brought up, she suddenly felt relieved. She'd been carrying it for too long by herself, and obsession or no, Crespi would have to understand—what it was like to be in the dark, and how important it was to take action, to find the truth no matter the cost.

Crespi stared at her for a long moment. She waited, calmer than she would have thought possible; David would have been proud of her . . .

"Lennox was stupid to send you coded information," he said, his voice low and angry. "And you're *supremely* stupid to be here on your own little fact-finding mission."

She felt stunned. Five minutes before, she had expected a response like that, felt *resigned* to it. But damnit, hadn't he heard a word she'd said? Her motives weren't based on *nothing;* who the hell did he think he was, judging her motives while asking her to dig for *him*? Anger flashed, hot and quick, and she had to struggle to keep from shouting.

"I've done a little fact-finding for *you*, don't forget! Are you interested in what I found out, or would you rather stay there on your throne and wait for your friend *God* to drop it in your lap?"

Crespi held up his hands, his cheeks flushed. "Easy, keep your voice down."

She glanced around the cafeteria, felt her anger dwindle as quickly as it had come. No one was watching, or had even looked up.

Crespi dropped his hands and then looked away from her, out into the void. "I—sorry, Lieutenant. What did you find?"

She brushed her hair away from her face and after a moment nodded. "Alright. First of all, I couldn't trace the station order that released that drone. There's a coded master record, but I don't know if I can crack it, it's real dirty.

"Second, all the crew members' medical records have been altered. No telling why 'til I bust that code."

Crespi frowned, leaned closer. "Do you have a number for crew fatalities?"

McGuinness nodded. "Hold on to your hat. Thirty-four in the last three years."

Crespi's eyes widened. "That's impossible!"

"Don't I wish."

"Eleven a year? And only one shuttle here and back a year? How? I mean, where are the replacements coming from?"

McGuinness crossed her arms, her manner conversational. "Maybe they're coming in on the three unscheduled shuttles that have been arriving each year for the past *five* years. It's all in the station mainline. Whatever's been going on here has support from high up."

Crespi's shock was somehow deeply gratifying.

"Son of a prick," he whispered.

"Do you want me to continue, in my supremely stupid way, to try to get into the master record? Sir?"

Crespi seemed to mentally shake himself, return his attention back to her. "McGuinness, I apologize for that. Yes, by all means continue."

"Thank you, sir."

He nodded, seemed to hear her own apology in her softened tone. "I don't need to tell you to be damn careful when you're looking. But if you're caught, I'll back you."

She let out a deep breath, suddenly grateful to this man for more than she could admit, even to herself. She hadn't realized how great a burden it had been, or how great her fear of being left out of the solution; David hadn't had any family, only her . . .

A drifting movement outside, far below the window. McGuinness peered down, made out the shape of—

"Oh!"

It was a body bag.

"Mortenson," she whispered, and Crespi followed her gaze out into the darkness.

For a moment they stood, watched the lone shape as it gently floated out beyond the station's light into its cold, airless tomb.

"Don't get caught, McGuinness," said Crespi, and then turned and walked out before she could think of anything to say.

12

Crespi took a deep breath, held it, and pushed the handles of the press machine up slowly. His arms trembled; sweat ran in rivulets down and across his neck. Final rep, second set, and he could feel the strain across his shoulders and back, the low, spreading ache that meant he was doing good—

He exhaled and brought the weight down, forcing the air out gradually between clenched teeth.

"Ten," he rasped, and released the handles. Not bad, considering. The stimulators in the sleep chambers were adequate, but some atrophy was inevitable—though he was almost back to pressing his own body weight, closer than he could've hoped so soon after the deep sleep.

He lay there for a moment, catching his breath, and

thought about what McGuinness had told him. Thirty-four crew members dead. How many had been connected to Church's research? He'd said none, but had they all died of heart attacks? Impossible.

No, Church was holding back and it looked like Thaves had to be involved; there was no way that that many could be kept a secret.

And why not? You wouldn't have known without McGuinness's prying—and it's still a secret to the brass back home . . .

Was it? Crespi considered and rejected the idea in a few seconds. Conspiracy theories were fine for fiction, but this was real life. Besides, if the Corps were in on it, they wouldn't bother running their tests way the hell out here, or with civilian techs; they'd keep it closer to home, and with their own people.

Church. He was decidedly eccentric, but was he so flat-out nuts that he would *kill* human beings for the sake of his research? He was working on telepathic communication between man and alien in order to *save* people. And what the hell would he do with a slew of corpses anyway?

Then there was Mortenson. It seemed probable that he had been murdered—but why? Had he stumbled across something he shouldn't have?

Crespi sighed deeply and ran his hand through his sweat-soaked hair. Too many questions, and the only answers didn't make much sense.

Unless . . .

Sharon McGuinness. Her story about David Lennox rang true, and it was a reasonable motive to dig—but he only had her word that any of this was going on. Her word and an old snapshot that showed her standing with a colonel doctor, who she *claimed* was Church's old assistant . . .

He rejected that one, too. His gut instinct was that she was one of the good guys on this, and her angry outburst back in mess cinched it for him; he would've done the same thing if his lover had died under such mysterious circumstances, damn the consequences. And he also would have mouthed off to anyone who berated him for it.

So what was happening aboard the *Innominata*? There were too many pieces missing to even hazard a guess, but what he had so far didn't smell too good. In fact, it stank out loud.

He sat up and reached for a towel, glancing at the clock set into the wall. It was a decent gym, he'd sweated plenty. He was ready for a shower, maybe a bite, and then he'd meet with Church, maybe feel him out about Mortenson's death. He didn't want the doctor to know what he had so far, the rest of it, but a little scoping might yield something useful . . .

Outside in the corridor, a woman screamed in terror.

Crespi jumped up from the bench and snatched his gym bag as the cry was joined by others.

"Run! Get away!"

"Oh, my God—"

Where, where is it— Crespi dug through the bag frantically, past toiletries and clothing. His hand wrapped around the machine pistol and then he was running, out into the passageway.

"Get it away. Oh, God, *keep it back!*"

Crespi charged into the hall, aimed at the center of the commotion, heart pounding—

And froze. It was Paul Church, smiling. Holding a leash.

With an alien drone at the other end.

Church sang to the little drone as they walked down the level B corridor, a song he only half remembered from his youth. Mostly he hummed, throwing in the few words he recalled when they seemed appropriate.

"Hey, day, diddley ummm, the cat and spoon ... mm-mm, dog eats moon ..."

The creature scrabbled frantically for purchase at the slick floor, its cries muffled by the metal harness's bit. Church gripped the extended and insulated handle in one hand, the "discipline" cord in the other. Each time the drone veered away from him, Church tapped the cord's switch, delivering a heavy electric jolt through the contraption.

It worked *perfectly;* the metal casing enveloped both the shoulders of the writhing drone and ran down the length of its spine, forcing it into a four-legged walk. A welded rod extended from each shoulder and met in front of the jaws, where it curved inward to effectively muzzle the beast. Of course, there *was* a slight drooling problem, but some things couldn't be helped. They'd certainly be easy to track, though ...

"Just follow the puddles, eh, Trix?"

He called over his shoulder to Blackman, who followed along from a distance. "Don't slip! Our doggie seems to be quite—salivous this morning!"

The drone tried another lunge forward and Church shocked it, frowning. "Bad! No!"

The voltage wasn't as high as he'd installed in the kennels, certainly—taking the beast for a drag was *not* what he'd had in mind. No, it was a—a *love* tap, just a hint of debilitating pain, enough to keep little Trixie on its toes, so to speak.

They passed a few people in the corridor, most of whom grew pale and disappeared quickly in spite of Church's reassuring demeanor. He wasn't surprised, really, though it was regretful; drones could be quite nasty, given the correct circumstances.

But not today, Trixie. You're mine *today.*

The sense of power was amazing, and Church felt almost high with it. It was his first attempt at harnessing one of the creatures, forcing it to his will while still being close enough to smell its acrid, musky scent. There was no question of who was in control, none whatsoever, although the few passing faces seemed to think differently.

Let them think what they will. In the end, I still hold the reins and you're still crawling in front of me.

They turned the corner and headed down corridor 5, where the station's small exercise room was. Crespi had mentioned a workout; perhaps he'd still be there, would see what Church was doing, and would forget all that sub rosa silliness with the McGuinness woman. How could a man, a *scientist* no less, care about piddling secrets when the power of the beast was right in front of him?

"Hey little blue, there in the corn ... mm-mm ... better hide your laugh and dog eats moon ..."

There was a woman tech midway down the passage, kneeling at a control panel set into the floor. Church gently steered the drone to the other side of the hall so as not to upset her, but they were only a few meters away before she happened to look up.

And screamed to wake the dead.

A few others farther along the corridor turned and saw the situation—then added to the false alarm by adding their own panicked voices.

Church cringed. Couldn't they *see*, were their eyes shadowed so heavily by their own prejudice?

The silly, screaming woman had backed herself against the wall and now pleaded for Church to take it away. He sighed heavily.

"Don't be afraid of Trixie, ma'am, he won't bite—"

She didn't seem to hear him, too caught in her own hysterical drama, lost in the sound of her own high-pitched complaints.

A burst of movement ahead, and his drone strained at the leash; someone had run into the hall, pointed a weapon at them.

Church grinned. Crespi, of course, all pumped up and drenched in a manly sweat. The look on the poor man's face was priceless.

He lowered his weapon and his words carried clearly to Church's ears.

"What the *fuck*—"

The drone suddenly lunged again, no doubt agitated by Crespi's offensive stance. Church zapped it, felt that small burst of pleasure as the creature writhed, its cries strangled and weak beneath the muzzle.

"*Bad*," he said again.

Crespi's stunned silence didn't last. He moved closer to Church (though not *too* close), and practically shouted in anger.

"What in the holy hell are you *doing*?!"

Wasn't it obvious? "Just taking Trixie for a walk," he said, but he could see already that the humor in the situation wasn't reaching Crespi.

Crespi's face contorted into a snarl of rage. "A—a walk?! I should arrest you on the spot!"

Church frowned. "Arrest me? What for?"

"What for? How about improper handling of contraband life forms, reckless endangerment, felony jeopardization? Conduct unbecoming to an officer? How about criminal *insanity*?!"

Church was taken aback. "I—was trying to make a point," he began, but Crespi cut him off.

"What in the name of Buddha could *that* be?"

Church suddenly felt a bit angry. "That I have these creatures completely under my control," he said coolly. "That they offer no threat."

Crespi still looked furious. "Tell that to Mortenson."

God, did Mortenson die just so it could be thrown in Church's face? "He was a fool who got himself killed by being where he had no business being."

Church turned around, found Blackman standing with a few other watchers. "Blackman, prepare the holding cell."

"Yes, sir."

He wheeled the drone around and started back to the kennel, the crew members scattering from the alien's path.

Crespi obviously had no imagination and no appreciation for the simple, pleasurable benefits of his research; that would have to change if they were going to be working together, but would he ever overcome his tendency toward emotional reaction?

"Looks like we'll have to teach him a few things," he whispered, but the alien paid no mind. It drooled and lunged, its talons scratching grooves into the worn passage floor beneath it.

Church sighed and depressed the buzzer again.

13

McGuinness came to his room late that night. Crespi was already in bed and half asleep.

"Come in," he said. Maybe she had some more information, a key to the strangeness of this place.

"Sorry to come by this late, but I wanted to talk to you about some things."

He sat up, turned on the small light by his bed. He usually slept in his boxers, so his chest was exposed. He started to reach for an undershirt, but she shook her head.

She sat down next to him and smiled, somewhat shyly. Her hair was down and looked thick and dark, beautiful. It surrounded her face, framed the sweet smile and clear, unlined skin.

He suddenly found it hard to talk; his throat was dry. "Lieutenant—"

"Sharon, please."

"Um. Sharon. Was there something in particular? That you wanted to, uh, discuss?"

She kept her gaze on his, and her tone was light—but as she spoke, her hands went to the front of her shirt and she began to untab it, exposing creamy skin.

"No, not really. I just wanted to know if we understood each other earlier, about why I'm here and why you're here. I loved David, but David's gone now, and I haven't been made love to in a long time. Will you? Make love to me?"

Crespi was literally speechless. He reached out, perhaps just to touch her hair, and she took his hand in both of hers and placed it gently on one breast. He groaned at the feel of it, the rounded weight of her flesh, and felt himself get hard beneath the blankets.

She leaned over and across him and turned out the light. The room was pitch-black, her breath warm across his lips.

They kissed, a long, wet moment, and then she pulled away. He could hear the sound of clothes being dropped to the floor, the faint hiss of her breath.

Hiss.

"Sharon?" The sound frightened him, so familiar—

The hissing grew louder, deeper. Not her voice at all, but another, furious, suddenly raising up to a high-pitched shriek of piercing intensity.

Crespi reached his hand outward, forward—

And felt the cold, hard shell, the spindly blackness of the creature's arm.

"Colonel Doctor Crespi," it croaked—

He sat up in the dark, choking back a scream.

"Colonel Doctor Crespi?"

The com. Church. On the intercom.

Dream, a dream, thank God— His gun was in his right hand, the metal barely warm from his body heat. He'd fallen asleep holding it.

—the creature's arm—

Crespi fumbled quickly for the light as Church spoke again.

"Colonel Doctor—"

"Yeah. Church?" His head was fuzzy, the last terrible image from the dream still clear. He set the weapon aside, not wanting to touch it anymore.

"Yes, it's Church. Sorry to disturb you—but the alien is dying. I thought you might want to be on hand."

Crespi nodded. "Oh ... yes, I would. I'll be right there."

The com went dead.

Crespi got out of bed and started to get dressed, glancing blearily at the clock. He'd been asleep for less than an hour, but it was just as well that Church had called; he didn't think he'd be able to sleep for quite some time.

Five minutes later he stood in front of the lab, yawning. His eyes felt gritty and his muscles ached from his earlier workout, but he felt surprisingly alert, all things considered.

The two guards waved him through with no hassle, the mandatory bioscan accompanied by friendly nods; Church must have told them that he was expected.

Crespi stepped onto the viewing ramp, saw Church

at the far end, his arms resting on the railing. The doctor didn't turn as Crespi walked out to meet him.

The drone lay on the floor of the enclosure in a pool of green-tinted saliva, not moving. It was curled into a fetal position and was so still that for a moment Crespi thought it was already dead.

The alien opened its jaws then and its inner set of mandibles slowly inched out, rested finally on the cold floor.

"What's it dying of?"

Church sounded tired. "Who knows? Too long away from the hive, too long away from the queen. Discouragement. Old age. In captivity they just die, as I told you. They just die."

Absurdly, Crespi felt an urge to comfort the aging doctor; he seemed depressed at the drone's imminent decease, almost despondent.

"Look at it, Crespi. Does your heart know this monster? Do you see the desperate fear of your fathers in its blind destroyer's head?"

Crespi didn't know what to say. Church's voice had taken on a musing tone, as if he were speaking his thoughts as they occurred.

"When men first looked into the outer void, into space, they looked into the soul of this soulless creature. When men kill each other, and hurt their children, and close their eyes so that good will not distract them, they are worshipping this creature."

Crespi studied the unmoving drone, his tired mind struggling to hold on to his hatred of the thing—but it looked pathetic, huddled on the floor like a giant, squashed bug, dying slowly in a puddle of its own drool.

Church continued in that low, thoughtful tone. "In

their hearts, all men would like to be like this creature—hideously strong, unchained by conscience, charged by the black heart of the cosmos to go forth and annihilate . . ."

Church bowed his head. "Good-bye, you dark thing." His voice was now only a whisper.

Crespi still couldn't think of anything to say. Church seemed honestly upset, a far cry from his somewhat indifferent manner over the death of Mortenson. That Church admired the alien breed was undeniable, if perhaps a bit odd; yesterday he had neatly sidestepped the question, but Crespi now wondered about Church's previous experience with the creatures; why would he choose to work with them?

Why would you, *Crespi?*

He frowned. *To change things for the better, to enlighten—*

Oh, really? And your conscience has nothing *to do with it?*

He couldn't answer that.

A suited lab technician called up from the main floor. "It's a flatliner, sir."

Church seemed to snap out of his trance. "Thank you, Stockdale. Have the body brought to B lab, please."

Crespi found his voice. "Now what?"

Church met his gaze finally. "Now comes the dissection."

He turned and walked back down the ramp, and Crespi followed, trying to convince himself that it was just his imagination, just the light—Church's eyes couldn't have been brimming with unshed tears.

*   *   *

Twenty minutes later Church stood in front of the drone's body and waited for Crespi to finish suiting up and join him. Stockdale waited by the instrument tray nearby, his face hidden by the mask filter and the protective goggles that Church also wore.

The lab was small, the computer system only adequate, but it had the cleanest light on board the station, as well as the only alloyed equipment tables. The brightness somehow diminished the creature that lay before him, stole away its very *dark* essence—but then, death had surely taken its own toll . . .

He sighed, looking down at the corpse. His moment of melancholy was past, the drone was dead and now there was work to be done—but watching them falter always gave him pause. That such a magnificent machine should will itself to die . . . it seemed so unnecessary. Sad.

Crespi walked into the lab, suited and ready. Church started explaining as soon as he reached the table.

"Its body acids have been drained and replaced with neutralizing agent. Still, we never know what we might run into; a little pocket of hot juice, a spurting gland."

He glanced at Crespi. The acid-resistant coverall fit him well. "I hope this protective gear isn't too cumbersome."

Crespi's eyes indicated a smile. "On the contrary, it's amazingly unconfining. Your own design?"

Church smoothed his own dark green suit, pleased. "Yes. The well-known mother of invention was my muse. Stockdale, hand me the Bretz saw, please."

"Yessir."

Crespi leaned closer as Church turned the nearly

silent cutter on and began to edge it through the creature's skull. He ran the saw up the right side of the thick cranium and back down, cutting a piece as wide as his hand and slightly over half a meter long.

"Ever seen inside one of these, Crespi?"

The doctor shrugged. "Only freshly blasted."

Church grinned as he turned the Bretz off and pried at the cut piece. "How very gung-ho of you."

He placed the strip aside and Crespi leaned in. Church pointed at a small, somewhat shriveled kidney-shaped organ near the front of the cavity, swimming in a spongy, gray-green swamp of chemicals.

"This organ is what interests me most."

Crespi frowned. "What is it?"

Church smiled. *Bait, Crespi! Let's see if it's tasty, shall we?*

"The surface is lined with compound cells of Fullerite-encased Hurlantium. The internal structure is solid neurons in two binary fans, very, very dense."

Crespi nodded, eyes sharpening, motioning for Church to go on.

"I think it's the alien 'psychic receiver,' so to speak. The Fullerite and Hurlantium pick up E-waves and the fans create interference patterns from electromagnetic fields."

Crespi was finally showing interest. "So it would not only receive brain waves, but enable the alien to assess physical characteristics by seeing its—subtle body."

Church smiled again. Not bad, not bad at all. "Exactly. That's why strong EM fields affect them so greatly. I imagine it gives them the equivalent of . . . an ice-cream headache."

Crespi seemed almost excited. "I'll remember that."

Church pointed to the organ again. "Now, you can see that this thing has withered. In healthy specimens, it's more bulbous, fills the cavity tightly. But in a languishing captive, it atrophies."

Crespi pounced. "Which would explain why the crewman under the influence of the telepathine was able to affect the drone's behavior!"

"Exactly. Stockdale, the Linnel?"

Church used the small, diamond-edged scalpel to slice through the sinewy gray strands that held the organ in place. He placed it in an alloyed pan and set in on one of the chest-level trays nearby.

Crespi switched on one of the small, intense spotlights above the tray and studied it closely. Church waited.

Come on, Crespi, it's right in front of you!

"If your surmisal is correct, this—receiver is where the crewman tuned in . . ."

Crespi stiffened, looked at Church with wide eyes.

By Jove, I think he's got it!

"Wait! Fullerite and Hurlantium can be synthesized!"

Church tried not to sound as patronizing as he suddenly felt. "It seems so obvious, doesn't it?"

Crespi was practically leaping with enthusiasm. "Have you tried to reconstruct it in a cold tank? Or computer model?"

"Not yet. The molecular structure is too complicated to be duplicated through traditional gelidification."

"What about the computer model?"

Church shook his head. "So far, I don't have sufficient structural data."

"Well, let's get it and build one of these things!"

Ah, the magic word! Crespi was hooked, no question, nothing left but to reel him in.

" 'Let's'? Does that mean you no longer consider this an illegal operation, Colonel Doctor?"

Crespi didn't hesitate. "It means I consider this research too important not to receive full attention."

Church smiled, glad that his mask kept Crespi from seeing it.

"Well, let's get back to work, then. And prepare yourself for a long haul, this may take hours."

He went back to the table, pointing out various organs and structures in the alien's body, labeling them for Crespi's grasping mind as the morning hours stretched on.

Crespi was as good as caught, cooked, and eaten. With a little luck, he'd have no more trouble from this man.

And perhaps, just perhaps . . . you've found the assistant you've been waiting for.

McGuinness sat in front of her computer screen and watched the bizarre autopsy, hoping that no late-night hackers were checking out the surveillance system. She'd crossed and redirected the image several times, but a good compweaver wouldn't have too much trouble tracing it—if they were looking for something specific, anyway.

She yawned, glanced absently at the small personal she borrowed from storage, still running its numbers against the ones she'd plugged in from the mainline. It bleated occasionally from its spot next to her cup of cold coffee, the soft tone of systems running through its tiny chip mind.

She looked back at the green-suited figures on the monitor. The voyeuristic feeling was a bit unnerving, but she meant to keep track of Church if she could. Crespi, too, for that matter. He seemed a little too excited by the alien dissection; could mean a loss of objectivity, and she didn't want to be the only one watching.

Doctor Church had taken one of his aliens out into the station earlier; it had been the talk of the rec room and again over dinner. If her suspicions were correct, that Church *had* been involved with David's death, the reason was becoming apparent, the evidence fitting together into a picture of undeniable clarity—Paul Church was insane.

She thought about David for a moment, their too-short time together, and then quickly pushed it away. From the day she'd decided to come to the *Innominata*, she hadn't allowed herself the leisure of grief. And wouldn't allow it now, not when she'd found out so much.

She wondered vaguely what he would think of her now—hell, what *anyone* would think. A woman obsessed, poking through matters that she probably had no business with.

Sure, obsession's the word, and it doesn't matter. Because nothing matters anymore except for what I can find to bring Church down.

The personal beeped again, an end signal, and she reached over to tap through the extensive list it presented. It took a few minutes to get through, consumption records, power placement—

Her heart seemed to stop in her chest. She went back to the beginning, read it again. A third time.

McGuinness laughed, high and shaky, looked back at the surveillance monitor and picked out Church.

"Got you, you bastard," she whispered, and hoped to God that she was right.

14

Crespi looked exhausted, but he had that happy, glazed look that told Church things couldn't have gone better. They walked through the lab, past Stockdale, meticulously cleaning the equipment. It was still another hour until "dawn," when the station's light would cycle up to full power.

"—and if we can use one more specimen I can get sixteen different models on re-quad, no problem."

Church struggled to get his lab coat on as Crespi babbled, full of ideas and propositions. The younger scientist seemed to have that boundless, wired energy that came from too little sleep.

Church smiled tiredly. "We'll start on the next shift, if you like."

Crespi smiled. "Excellent, excellent. The implications of this project are mind-numbingly significant, Doctor."

Church fixed him with a serious gaze. "I quite agree. And if I may say so, it takes a special kind of scientist to appreciate that."

Crespi smiled and nodded shortly, accepting the compliment without fluster.

And without seeing it for what it is . . .

"Why don't you go get some rest, eh? You look all done in."

Crespi shrugged, grinning. "Right, though I don't know if I'll be able to sleep. See you in eight hours."

He veered down the corridor back toward his quarters, and Church went toward his own. His room was located next to one of the smaller, unused labs, on the station's industrial level. It was quieter there, more private, and he liked feeling that he was the only man alive down there . . .

He took the lift down and walked to his quarters, yawning. He was bone-weary, too old to be staying up all night. Not that his body couldn't function, but his mind grew distant, hazy.

In spite of his exhaustion, he knew it would be a while before sleep came. He'd been suffering a mild insomnia for several months, perhaps from the excitement of his research. He'd made quite a few breakthroughs since he'd started the experiments, and felt that he was coming closer to his quest with each day.

Did Crespi understand? That seemed to be the question, didn't it? False flattery aside, the man *was* quite capable, if somewhat limited; there was no reason for Church to dismiss him, certainly, he seemed to grasp many of the minute details that previous assistants had not. But would it be enough? Did he dare to hope . . . ?

Sleep now.

He entered the dark room and went to the small kitchen area, where he kept a few assorted drugs—sleep enhancers, caffidrine pills, and the like. He tapped a glass of water and downed two of the sleeping tablets before heading back into the dim bedroom.

Church removed his shoes and glasses, then lay back to wait for the pills to kick in.

Funny, how seeing the drone die had stirred up such emotion; he usually felt something like regret, even pity—but the feelings that had rushed over him earlier had been intensely unhappy ones, bitterly nostalgic. He didn't like to think of the . . .

(hell)

. . . time that his family had stopped on that small moon, it was pointless and painful. But there were times he couldn't help it, couldn't hold back the flood of memories that he'd worked so hard to dam. Most had faded with time, the emotions muted, the times and chronology misplaced . . .

Church closed his eyes, helpless to stop himself as the sleep tablets rushed through his system.

There were some things he'd never forget.

The aliens jerked and pulled the stumbling humans through the low brush of Eden, away from the Genesis station and their ship.

"Paul? Paul!" His mother was somewhere ahead of him, couldn't see that he was still there.

"Okay!" he shouted, though he felt anything but okay. The monster that held him did so with incredible strength; his arms were already bruised and aching, and he knew, with no trace of doubt, that they were all being taken to their deaths.

Why haven't they killed us already? Why would they—

A sudden, sick dread filled him. Those stories they'd heard back on that military station—the aliens used humans for more than food, used them for . . .

Paul struggled harder against the merciless claws, but the creature gripped tighter, hissing. Small rivulets of blood ran down his arms as the talons pierced his skin.

Ahead, a huge rock, overgrown with weeds and green moss, easily as big as their ship. Bigger. As they got closer, Paul could see that it wasn't a rock at all. And the smell—

It was the source of the fetid scent he'd noticed earlier. An odor of decay, of mold, and a strange, sour musk like nothing he'd ever smelled before. It was of rotten flesh, dying sweat, of boiling vomit and flat, poisonous chemicals. He knew he'd never be able to describe it to someone who didn't already know it, and he realized at the same time that he probably wouldn't survive to . . .

They hadn't seen the hive when they'd landed because of the vegetation all over it. A stupid, possibly fatal mistake—because the drones had seen *them*, probably watching from their rancid nest, hissing and shrieking in mad pleasure—

"Everybody try and stay calm! They're not going to kill us right away, we've still got—"

His father's voice was cut off as the creature that carried him shoved him toward an opening at the base of the hive, a dark, ragged hole. One by one, Paul's family and friends were pushed through the opening, followed and led by the hissing drones.

Paul was last, and he could hear the choked moans of the others as the stench hit him. It was *beyond* stench, a foul miasma that raped his lungs and burned his eyes and throat. He tried to breathe shallowly, through his mouth, but the air tasted almost as brutal as it smelled.

He heard the sound of someone throwing up, Louise Clark, and he thought insanely that the creatures would stop, let her clean herself up—

No. That was the thought of a human mind, a civilized gesture that meant less than nothing in this place. He had to stop, try to see past his panic, and accept that this was happening; to do less was to invite insanity . . .

The drone dragging him along caught up to the rest, where he could see their pallid faces in the dim, murky light, contorted with terror and pain. Louise was drenched in vomit and drew in deep, ragged breaths, the bile still trickling from her chin.

The journey probably lasted only a minute or so, but it felt like forever, a twisted, terrifying jaunt through a haunted cavern. Strange, misshapen ropes of dark secretion hung from the walls, the bizarre symmetry as alien as the creatures themselves. The walls had hollow places, pits, from which black, grinning heads peered out to study the new arrivals, chittering in flashes of shining, wet teeth.

They were brought to some kind of open chamber and dumped unceremoniously on the ground, the high walls stretching up into the stinking darkness like a cathedral of bones. His parents crowded around him, as Rebecca's did for her—as if they could protect their children in this place, keep them from harm. Judith stepped up to Paul's father.

"Can you defend us?" His voice was shaky and frightened.

Even she seemed pale in the gloom, the only light filtered through webbed cracks high above. "If they attack."

Lucian Church had started to cry. "They *have*, don't you see that? Can't you kill them?"

Judith shook her head. "I will defend you to the best of my abilities, but I probably won't cause any damage before they stop me."

The drones had pulled back for a moment, but now they came closer, crept forward with their arms outstretched.

It was hopeless, there were too many of them. Paul spun around wildly, frantic for a way out, but there was none; cracks and fissures high above seemed to mock them, casting faint, sweet light from Eden so far away ... there was only murk and hissing monsters and the promise of impregnation, their bodies used to incubate the alien young, a cruel, living torture before death. And that horrible, horrible stink. If they made it out of this, he'd never forget it, or what it felt like knowing that hope was sometimes all one had.

Never—

He slept, dreaming that the sun had died, casting an eternal darkness over all the worlds that man had ever known.

15

Crespi was getting un-
dressed for bed when someone buzzed at his door.

"Who is it?"

"Lieutenant McGuinness, sir."

"Just a moment."

He quickly pulled his pants back on, and after a
slight hesitation, grabbed for his overshirt. He had almost forgotten his dream from the night before, but
her cool voice over the com reminded him.

He buttoned up and ran his hands through his hair.
"Come in."

McGuinness stepped into his quarters looking nothing like she had in his unpleasant dream; her hair was
tied back, her face strained and sleepy. Still, he felt almost embarrassed just looking at her.

The smooth, full weight of her breast in his hand, her agile tongue—

Whoosh. As if that didn't make things awkward enough, they were also going to have to clear a few things up about Church. And considering her emotional investment in the search, he might have to fall back on rank. He kept his tone controlled and official.

"What is it, Lieutenant?"

"I've found out something very important, about Church and—"

"So have I, McGuinness." He smiled gently at her and hoped that she would listen and understand.

"I've just spent six hours watching Colonel Doctor Church in action; the man is, to use a much abused term, a genius. The work he's doing here will change the face of science forever."

McGuinness frowned. "But—"

He cut her off again; she wasn't getting it. "I realize you had personal motivations, but Church is a total professional. As of this moment, you will desist spying around. Understood?"

The lieutenant remained calm, her voice steady. "Sir, I've been pirating the station surveillance system. I've followed Church's every move for the last eighteen hours, I watched you and him dissect the alien—"

Crespi sighed. He was going to have to make it a direct order, perhaps even limit her access to the mainline. It was unfortunate, really, he liked the lieutenant well enough—

—and maybe more, Doctor, don't you think?

—but this had to stop. Church was opening doors to technological innovation that bordered on the *mystical*, true breakthroughs into—

Her sharp, pleading tone cut his thoughts off. "Listen to me! He's toying with you, sir. The alien research is only a small part of what he's doing here; the station resource requirements don't jibe with consumption records, do you understand? They don't match up. Something on board the *Innominata* is using a third again as much power as all known systems, *including* the alien lab, combined."

It took a few beats for her words to sink in. Crespi felt a slow but unstoppable shock course through him, but he still struggled to stay on top, not wanting to believe her. "But what Church is doing, that would take up a lot . . ."

McGuinness shook her head. "He has a hidden operation on board. Something big that he doesn't want you to find. He's engaged your interest in the alien research to throw you off track; it's all on the record, sir, you can look for yourself."

Was it possible? He thought about Church's strange smiles, the odd lapses at the autopsy, the sidestepping. The compliments . . .

He turned his head, closed his eyes. Instinct. Goddamnit, *instinct!*

Church is still holding back; you know it.

Crespi *did* know it.

Maybe.

He looked back at the lieutenant, waiting patiently for his response. He felt uncertain, but McGuinness had been straight with him so far—and Church *had* lied about the crew fatalities, or at least it seemed. If he'd been tricked . . .

It had to be true, she said there was proof.

He felt a cold, sudden hatred for Church, and a

sudden warmth of gratitude to the woman who stood in front of him.

"McGuinness, you're a good soldier. Do you know where this ghost facility is?"

She seemed relieved, the small lines of tension in her face melting away. "I think so, sir. I believe it's located in K lab, down on his drone maze level. It's designated as a zero-G facility, but that's where the thirty percent power overage is going. Church has had three double-code, single-access lock doors installed, and it's not on the station mainline at all."

Which means no one can get in but Church.

"My name's Tony," he said absently. "Okay, you've convinced me. How do we get in?"

McGuinness grinned tightly. "Church has a code slate. If we can get that, I can extract the key. I saw him leave it on his private console in his unity office."

Crespi nodded. "Where is he now?"

"Took something. He should be out like a light by now."

He took a deep breath. "Can you get the slate?"

"The bioscan won't let me in. You'll have to do it."

Crespi hesitated, his brief certainty now wavering. This wasn't concept, it was a reality—he would have to take action. If McGuinness was telling the truth, he had no choice. It almost certainly meant the end of Church's research, if he was doing something so illegal that it was being hidden from the Corps—and that would be an immeasurable loss of time and effort, his work with the alien telepathy wasted. There would be years of red tape before it could be started up again, if it *ever* was.

And if he got caught—if she was lying . . .

You'll know soon enough, won't you?

Crespi spoke quickly, sounding calmer and more controlled than he felt. "Stay here, I'll be right back. Use my private com line if anything comes up."

She nodded mutely and he turned and walked out, before he could change his mind.

After Crespi left, McGuinness sighed, sagged down onto the rumpled bed, and lay back. It had been a long couple of days, and she was exhausted. The sheets smelled pleasantly masculine, comforting scents from her time with David—soap and clean sweat, and also an odor that was distinctly Tony's—

She closed her eyes, smiled sadly. *That's* Colonel *Tony to you, Lieutenant.* David was still too close. And she wasn't ready, at least not until this was over with.

Although you could *ask him to call you Sharon . . .*

She sat up, half amused by her moot speculation. It wasn't the time, and definitely not the place. She looked at the clock on the wall, watched the seconds tick by, and wished Colonel Tony luck. He was probably going to need it.

Crespi hurried to the lift and then stepped out into the unfamiliar corridor, feeling angry and nervous. He hadn't been to Church's unity hole yet, though it wasn't technically off-limits; the office was centrally located, most of the main labs branching out from it.

Relax, the place should be deserted at this hour.

True enough. He felt stupid anyway, skulking around like some kind of thief—particularly if Church was hiding something. He had a right, a *duty* to find out the truth. He straightened his shoulders, hung a right at the end of the passageway. A small flight of stairs, then the office door.

He paused outside the heavily armored entry, and a fresh wave of anxiety flowed over him as he realized that he hadn't brought his piece. Not that he'd *need* it, necessarily, but not having it made him uncomfortable. What if—

What if what, Crespi? What if Church is lurking in there with a grenade launcher? Get the fucking slate and get on with it!

Crespi pressed his thumb into the indented hand plate and waited. In few seconds, the door swung open, leading through a small antechamber to another door.

The lights were dim, but the passage was empty; he felt his guts loosen, and he chided himself for acting like a fool. He strode to the second entry, which slid open to reveal a dark office, the only light coming through a window wall at the far end of the large room. Past that was a combination office/laboratory, and Crespi could see that the dim illumination came from a few monitors there, blinking softly.

Crespi's gaze darted to the main desk, littered with hard copy and empty coffee mugs. A hand-sized slate lay amid the clutter, on the keyboard of a small PC.

He walked over and picked it up, shoved it into his breast pocket.

See? Right where it was supposed to be, no fuss, no alarms, no armed Marines telling you to drop it—

He told his mind to shut up as he turned to leave the office. McGuinness would get the key; they could check out the private lab and get this whole covert business behind them—

He stopped, turned back to the darkness. Something stank. Maybe a tech had left their donut out too long, there was a definite rotten odor; he could at least throw the thing away, whatever—

Oh, no . . .

It had been a long time, but he knew that smell. Crespi froze, no sudden movements, but his brain screamed frantically, *Run, run, get the fuck out—*

A string of warmth fell from above, splattered delicately on one shoulder. He looked up slowly, his nuts crawling into his body, his heart suddenly in the pit of his stomach.

The drone above him shrieked. And jumped.

16

Crespi fell back, praying that it wouldn't land on top of him. He managed to stay on his feet and the drone dropped nimbly into a crouch, hardly a meter in front of him, teeth bared.

Hissing, it rose up, raised one massive, gleaming claw. Lightning fast, it backhanded Crespi, hurled him backward and into the wall of plexiglass.

It was old and brittle. He felt it give, shatter, and crash all around him as he was thrown roughly to the floor of the adjoining lab. Pain, but no time for it; he was up, stumbling, his only thought to find a weapon of some kind. The drone screamed in fury and leapt after him.

Gun stick rock anything—

He couldn't look back, wouldn't, knew he'd see the

grinning face of death right behind, claws outstretched, the stainless-steel teeth gnashing—

There! Past a slew of bolted chairs and desktops,
the room opened out, free space—and an electromag
field generator to one side, a portable, cords trailing
from it into hidden sockets.

Let it be on, ohgod—

A sudden pain in his ankle as he tripped across one
of the metal chair struts, not seeing it until too late.
He hit the floor hard, felt the drone *right behind*—

The fall saved him. The creature was seemingly
centimeters away, and it flew over him before it could
stop. Its claws scrabbled against the smooth floor as
it struggled to turn back.

To rip out his heart and eat it.

On the desk, something. He grabbed for it, an aerosol can, turned, and sprayed wildly as the monster
leapt for him.

A cloud of mist burst from the can, spattered into
the drone's descending maw. The creature shrieked in
pain and fury and jumped back, seemingly desperate
to escape the unknown spray.

Crespi yanked himself up, the can gripped tightly,
sweaty in his clutching fingers. He ran for the portable generator without looking at the drone, knew that
it would be prepared to strike again in seconds.

He felt blood from his cut face trickle down, into
his gasping mouth, and he spit bloody foam to one
side—

generator, electromag weapon kill—

—seeing only the portable, now a few meters away.

The control panel was at the base, on the floor, and
Crespi didn't hesitate. He hurled himself into a dive,
slid to it on his belly, and flipped over.

The drone was there, hissing, poised to leap from just two meters away. Crespi shouted, a wordless cry of intense frustration, and slammed his hand into the panel. Open. Hit a switch without looking, prayed that it was the right one.

The drone struck, the motion slowed in his mind's eye to a crawl, and Crespi snatched at the nearest cord, ripped it loose, pointing it at the creature as he jammed the button on the aerosol can again.

A bright spark of electricity from the cord, and the can's substance was aflame, spouting fire at the springing creature like a tiny incinerator. The drone recoiled, tried to pull back, but the fiery spray engulfed its long, slick head, spattered, and stuck to its exoskeleton like tar.

Screaming, it fell backward, limbs flailing at the substance. He had a second, maybe less—

Crespi jerked his wild gaze to the controls, *on,* he punched the power switch, the green button, the last second of his life—

A high-pitched hum, followed by a higher, louder scream.

The alien reeled back, brought its murderous claws to the sides of its smoldering head, screamed and screamed—

Before collapsing to the floor, unconscious.

Crespi drew in a long, ragged breath, and leaned back against the generator, too shocked to move, to think, to do anything but breathe. The echoes from the drone's cries still rang in his ears. From nearby, he heard running footsteps, frantic shouts.

He held up the mysterious can of fluid and read the label dully. Hair spray. It was hair spray.

He wanted to laugh but was afraid to open his

mouth, afraid of the hysteria that roiled up inside. Afraid that he would sob instead, and not be able to stop.

A young man in a baseball cap ran into the room, followed by another, both suited as electrical techs.

"What—Colonel Doctor Crespi!" That from the man in the cap. His face was pale, confused, sweaty with surprise.

The second man saw the creature and his own face went ashen. He stared at Crespi with something like awe. "Another one got out—?"

Baseball was already tapped into his com and now spoke rapidly. "Stockdale, we have an alien in the accentuator room near the unity. It's been 'magged, but you better get a full team down here, A and R."

Armed and ready, great, what was it doing *here?!*

The other tech, a burly blond man, still looked at Crespi, his dazed blue eyes full of something like wonder. "If you didn't—how did you—?" He shook his head.

"You're a lucky man, sir."

Lucky. I'm a lucky man— He raised one shaky hand to his face, felt the blood there, already tacky and starting to dry, the injuries minor. His back felt cut, too, and aching so badly that he didn't think he'd be able to walk the next day.

But he *was* alive. The drone was down, and he had survived; barely, but it was enough.

His shock ebbed for a second, and his thoughts found focus amid the daze of pain and confusion; it had happened so fast, been so unexpected—

Except someone had known about it. The someone who had sent him here to die.

Crespi stood, ignored the calls of the technicians as

they stuttered something about keeping still, ignored the bruised flesh that was already shrieking for rest, for relief. He stalked to the door and down the corridor with only one thought in mind, the only thing that made sense now.

That fucking *bitch*. He'd kill her.

17

McGuinness looked up eagerly as the door slid open, hoping that Crespi had gotten the code slate. He'd been gone longer than she thought he'd be, and she was starting to feel anxious, a dull ache of worry low in her gut.

He stood in the door then, and she spoke quickly, relieved to see him. "Did you get it, sir . . . ?"

She trailed off. He'd been in some kind of fight; his clothes were ripped in places, his grim face was bleeding. She opened her mouth to ask, see if he was all right—

He stalked across the room, right at her, and she saw at the last second that he didn't mean to stop.

Crespi grabbed at her shoulders, her clothes, and dug his fingers into her flesh, hard.

"No! What are you doing?!"

His hands went to her throat. He pushed her back, slammed her body up against the wall.

What the hell happened down there—

He was furious, his voice low and dripping with hatred. "You sent me down there to die, didn't you? *Didn't* you?!"

McGuinness struggled for air, clawed at his iron grip. "What are you—stop it, you're hurting me!"

His dark eyes were almost black with anger. "I'll hurt you, alright, I'll hurt you—"

His grip tightened, and dark shadows began to swim across her vision. She could barely speak now, her words choked and raspy. "Didn't—no, didn't—killing me . . ."

He suddenly let her go, and she fell to the floor, choking for air. His words seemed distant, far away.

"You set me up, McGuinness! You worthless traitor, I *should* kill you!"

McGuinness crawled to her hands and knees, raised herself up. "No," she whispered, and coughed, the sensation agonizing, but the confusion somehow worse. "No."

She looked up at him, and he must have seen the innocence in her face; he still glowered down at her, angrier than she'd ever seen a grown man, but he stopped shouting.

"I ought to shoot you on the spot. A fucking drone attacked me."

McGuinness felt shock, disbelief. He thought *she* had—

"No," she whispered, and the truth was suddenly a bright flash in her mind, the only answer. "It was Church. Had to be Church."

"You said he was *asleep*," he scowled.

She shook her head, helpless in her own dark astonishment. "I don't know, maybe before—"

Wait. A sudden, frantic hope. "Did you get the slate? Let me have it, I'll prove I'm right!" She stood up, the pain in her throat subsiding to a dull, pulsing ache. She held out her hand, waited, afraid that he might attack her again—or worse, that he wouldn't believe her.

His frown deepened, and she could see him try to sort it out, to decide. Uncertainty played across his bloodied features, a strange expression on his normally intense and focused face—but he dug into a front pocket and produced the slate. She reached for it, but he gripped it tightly, stared into her eyes, his own cold and hard.

"You get one chance to show me."

"I will, I swear I will."

He let go of the code slate and she felt a rush of cool relief. She *could* prove it, had no choice now but to unmask the facts; she turned for the door, eager to show him.

"Come on, let's get to K lab right now. Church will be notified about the attack, and he'll come looking for us."

Right now, that sounded a fuck of a lot scarier than any alien drone; if Church was that desperate, to unleash one of his creatures, there was no telling what he'd do when he found that Crespi was alive.

Crespi paused to grab his weapon, eyes unreadable now, and then they were out in the corridor, hurrying to the lowest level of the station. She wished vainly that she'd thought to bring her own weapon, but there was no time—and Crespi didn't look like he'd be willing to wait.

She held the slate tightly, afraid that she'd lose it somehow as they jogged through twisting corridors and into the lift that would take them to the secret lab.

This was her only chance. If she was wrong, there'd be hell to pay.

Crespi followed McGuinness through the still-dim passageways, his body aching with a pain he hadn't known in years and years. He was torn, uncertain, and he hated that even more than the physical suffering. But the worst . . .

I don't know who to trust anymore. His instincts were dead, he couldn't find his gut-center, the tiny voice that had always told him which path to take. He couldn't trust *himself;* he was too tired and too hurt to find his own way through this. He'd believed in her, and he had been wrong, hadn't he?

McGuinness said she could prove her story. And so he followed her, perhaps to his own death at her treacherous hands . . . or by Church's. Or some fucking drone, oblivious to the cares of men, not giving a shit for hope or loss or fear, not caring if you'd grown old and out of touch with what was real and what was smiling deceit—

And would that be so bad, Crespi? You've been living on borrowed time ever since that rock near Solano's moon, and you know it.

Suddenly it all came together, the memories, the nagging anxiety he'd felt from the moment out of deep sleep. He *did* know it, and had known deep down all along, no matter how he'd tried to bury the truth beneath his work—since he'd come here, it had all resurfaced, haunting him at every turn, refusing to be pushed away any longer. He'd made a career far away from that horrible morning, had let that fear fester in the darkness of his deepest heart—that he didn't deserve to be the only one left and someday there would be a price for it . . .

. Except here it was, finally; and the funny thing was, after avoiding it for so long, right now it didn't seem so scary after all. If there *was* a price to pay, now was as good a time as any—but maybe when it was your time to go, you just went. Maybe he'd stayed alive until he could understand that. And perhaps when you lost that little voice inside, you were just—done.

That's the spirit! Why don't you just give up now, save everyone else the trouble?

Fuck that shit; he was too tired, his mind was playing tricks. He stopped thinking and tried to concentrate on keeping up.

After an eternity of gloomy hallways and wrong turns, they stopped in front of a huge metal circle, an unlabeled door at the end of the lowest deck. The corridor was grimy, probably hadn't been cleaned in years, but the door was polished and gleaming. There were no handles, no bioscan, no guard—it looked solidly impenetrable. Only a small slot to one side, a slate plug.

McGuinness fumbled with the code slate, echoed his own thoughts aloud. "This is absolutely impassable without a key code—which we've got right here . . ."

He could see the finger-shaped bruises on her neck, and wondered if he should feel guilty, if she *was* innocent—he just didn't know.

Maybe that's *the price, Doctor. Maybe payment time has come.*

He had a sudden urge to shoot himself in the head, just to stop his brain from taunting him any longer. He laughed, a short bark of humorless sound; wouldn't that take the prize? He'd slayed the mighty dragon with a can of hair spray, just to off himself in a fit of existential angst. McGuinness looked at him nervously, but he shook his head and motioned for her to go on.

Hold on, not much longer—

She inserted the slate, frowned, punched a button. The door sighed open, swinging outward, revealing another door just inside.

She repeated the process. This one took two tries, but finally it opened into another small passage.

Last door. Crespi pulled his weapon, held it down but ready. He would go out fighting, at least. If it came to that.

The heavy door swung open in a rush of cool, moist air, revealing Church's private lab.

"No." McGuinness breathed the word that seemed to sum up the horrible impossibility of the place.

Crespi stepped forward, his weapon forgotten for the moment, everything forgotten; at last, the truth was painfully apparent.

Paul Church was hopelessly, irretrievably mad.

18

McGuinness stared around, eyes wide, and still she couldn't take it all in; her mind refused to accept what she was seeing.

"No, no, no, no . . ." Her own voice, quiet and disbelieving. Crespi said nothing, his face masked with dull shock.

The lab was small, smaller than most of the others on board the station, but still big enough to fit perhaps a hundred people—

Or thirty-four . . . Her mind tittered. She realized that hysteria was close to the surface, a mad, soul-rendering laughter that would turn to screams all too soon.

Traditional tables, monitors, computer pads scattered about—and clumped masses of cable leading into and out of tall vertical holding tanks, bubbling with some clear, viscous fluid. She turned away from them, not ready to comprehend the aberrant horrors inside; not *able* to.

On the nearest table to their left slumped the head-less corpse of what was once a heavyset man, tubes and cords running from every orifice. The figure was on its knees, the flaccid penis dangling limply above a wired cup that encased the scrotum. Where his head should have been, a misshapen metal plate, set with switches and a series of tiny, pulsing white lights. His back and chest were covered with dark hair and hundreds of small, lipless scars, some still recent, an angry red. The skin had ruptured at his upper back and twin, gleaming bone plates rose a few inches out of where his shoulder blades should have been.

The table next to it: another headless body, its belly swollen as if it carried a child, but no human child—the skin had burst in places, unable to accommodate the massive swelling, exposing the glistening red of muscle tissue. More tiny white lights, more switches. In spite of the obvious impregnation, the sex of the figure was unclear; there were no breasts, the entire chest area a mass of scar tissue, no genitalia apparent.

A tray between the tables held syringes, scalpels, a handheld laser cutter—and a small, blinking monitor and keyboard. McGuinness went closer, unable to stop, drawn to the obscenities as if in a terrible dream; she had to see what the monitor was for.

The two once-human figures stank of shit and bile as she stepped to the screen, read what was printed there—and moaned, a deep, hopeless sound born of sick revulsion and comprehension.

The computer listed their pulse rates; they were alive.

She backed away, still moaning, suddenly faint, twisted away from the undead abominations to run, to get away, *so cold here—*

Crespi was there. He reached out, wrapped his arms around her, and held her tight. She struggled, pushed at him, only vaguely aware that the awful, high-pitched mewls of terror and panic she heard were coming from her own throat.

He was speaking, but she couldn't hear, saw only the holding tank behind him, the naked, bubbling form inside, the strange, tumorous pink flesh that sprouted from all over it in loathsome tentacles, floating—

Crespi again, his pale face thrust into her own. ". . . at me! Look at me!"

She found his gaze then, saw the dark eyes filled with fear, with deep distress—and with acceptance.

"Lieutenant! Sharon! Deal with it, understand? *Deal with it!*"

She searched his eyes, saw the truth there, and nodded, swallowing. "I—okay, okay. Okay."

He let her go, gently, studying her face. She nodded again, took a deep breath. "I see it," she said, not even sure what she meant, but he nodded in return.

Together, they moved through the vault of horrors slowly, stopping between each abhorrent display, too sickened to move any faster to the next. Mutated alien embryos, dissected and labeled. A tangle of human limbs in a refrigeration unit. That strange alien musk, mingling with the scent of human feces and laboratory disinfectant in the damp, cold air . . .

The lab was L-shaped, the two of them still in the

front leg; McGuinness wanted out, badly, but knew that they had to see all of it, document the atrocities before they could be destroyed. These—*people* weren't truly alive; the machines were pumping blood and oxygen through their systems in a gross parody of life, forcing them to go on. She imagined that most if not all had been dead before they were brought here; tissue reanimation was nothing new. But what she wanted more than anything was to know *why*, why Church had done these things ... insanity was too mild a word, but she could think of no other.

What are words to this? How can there be a category for this to fit into in any language, any thought?

Four more tables, and three of the unmoving figures had heads, though limbs were missing, their flesh scratched and scarred seemingly without motive. The corpses were human, certainly—but their bodies had been twisted and re-formed, dark knobs and angles rising from breaks in the skin.

"Oh, God," whispered Crespi, and she turned, saw his attention fixed on one of the holding tanks, expression sick and appalled.

The submerged figure was male, naked, its light hair floating loosely around its pale, mutilated face—only the eyes were still whole, wide, the look there one of shock and disbelief.

Lieutenant Mortenson hadn't been jettisoned after all.

His exhaustion was probably the only thing that saved Crespi from losing it as they stepped into the lab—that, and his fight with the drone back in

Church's office. The day was already a surreal nightmare, and the additional horrors of Church's hidden facility somehow fit right in, embraced the atrocity that lay before them.

As it was, though, he felt right on the edge. McGuinness had helped stave off his own hysteria by losing touch for a moment—getting her back on track, having someone to watch for, had allowed him to see what was there, no matter how much his mind wanted to reject it.

Church was sick, deranged. Crespi searched for scientific reasons, desperate to make sense of the demented experiments—

Endorphin release? Telepathine work on reflexes, something like that?

Maybe. But it didn't explain the bizarre, tumorous growths that rose up from the flesh, the misshapen limbs, the atrocities in the liquid-filled tanks—

"Oh, God." His voice sounded faint and hoarse in the quiet, rife with horrified dismay.

Mortenson was suspended in one of the huge vats, his eyes wide and unseeing, unknown tubes and cords leading into and out of his pale, naked form. Slow, mutant bubbles rose around him, inching past his battered flesh and beginning again at his feet.

Crespi gagged suddenly, turned away, and then McGuinness was right next to him, her hand cool against his neck.

He closed his eyes, then nodded. "Okay. Let's finish and get the hell out of here."

McGuinness took his hand and they walked quickly to the end of the lab, turned to the right, started down a smaller room lined with blinking monitors. Nothing but humming computers, machines at work. Crespi felt a faint rush of gratitude—nothing more, no other horrors here, they could leave. He'd seen plenty.

Except—

At the very back of the room, a closed door like the three that guarded the lab, round and gleaming, partly open. And next to that, a thing that Crespi couldn't quite fit his mind around, it was so strange—

He stepped closer, paused, didn't feel McGuinness drop his hand as he studied the newest aberration.

The head and uppermost torso of a man, coming out of the far wall. Panels of circuitry surrounded him, the top of the head covered with a metal helmet—joined to an eye-level monitor beneath him by way of a long, snakelike metal arm, curling downward. That the young man had been dismembered was obvious; ragged strips of flesh hung down from the place where his chest joined the wall, cauterized and black.

That face . . .

Familiar somehow, but he couldn't place it. The stark lips were drawn back, exposing the man's even teeth in a gruesome, eternal grin. His once-blond hair, now dark and dust, flopped down across his smooth brow in lank waves. Even in death (and he *must* be dead, pulse or no) it was apparent that he was attractive, had once been a handsome man—

A low, keening wail just behind him. Crespi twisted around, startled. McGuinness stood there, her face contorted with some horrible pain, eyes bright with it, the sound of her cry long and anguished as she stared at the half man.

"What? What is it?" Crespi touched her, somehow more afraid than he'd been all along at the look of anguish in her wild eyes.

She collapsed against him, clutched desperately at his arms and back with clawing hands, buried her head against him as she screamed two words, over and over.

"It's David! It's David!"

19

The sleeping tablets had worked a bit *too* well, and Church felt truly out of sorts as he hurried down the corridor, turned toward the lab. The doors were standing open. As he'd assumed.

A nervous technician had woken him from a deep sleep with the news that another drone had escaped and had been found in the unity office, 'magged by Doctor Crespi—which meant that his Crespi knew more than he should, and that the lonely guard dog had been unable to stop him. Church had set up the "burglar alarm" months before, a time release on the kennel door, but he'd only used it a few times, back when David had started to ask too many questions . . .

The obvious conclusion was that Crespi had uncovered the secret that Church had successfully kept hidden from the entire station for over three years now; Thaves didn't even know, although Church figured the man had his suspicions. The admiral knew about the chemical work, of course, but as for the rest . . . ?

Church sighed, stepped through the hatches quickly. A shame, really, he had hoped for so much *better* from Crespi. The young doctor could have at least waited for an invitation; this was so informal, he would surely think the worst . . .

Church surveyed the room, looked for anything out of place. At least nothing had been tampered with. The conditions of his subjects were quite delicate; one clumsy move could upset their chemical readings for weeks, perhaps even taint the final results into uselessness. Just like that, half his work wasted—

A horrible cry from the back of the lab, piercingly loud. It certainly wasn't Crespi. Church sighed again. It was that woman, Mc-something-or-other, sounding more out of sorts than he felt.

He moved quickly toward the sound, somewhat annoyed. McGuinness, that was it. Why was *she* here? If only she'd had more incentive to search on her own, to break into his office without involving Crespi—

Now, don't get cross! You're just sleepy. The situation isn't a total loss, not if you can persuade Crespi to see reason.

He saw them as he turned the corner, the woman clutching at a very pale Crespi, screaming out David's name, over and again.

Church stood quietly for a moment, trying to assess the damage that had been done. Without explanation, his experiments *would* seem quite damning; this could take some talking.

He had to start somewhere. "For what it's worth,"

he said softly, "he's feeling no pain. Quite the contrary."

They both turned, their expressions priceless—they both looked as if they had expected death to be standing there, their eyes wide and mouths open in startled fear. When they saw only the small, aging scientist, their faces changed, became angry and somewhat confrontational.

Oh, dear—

The woman was first. She screamed, a wordless cry of rage and pain. She ran for him, her arms seeking to throttle, her teeth to rip and tear.

"I'll *kill* you!"

"No, you won't," he began, she had no weapon, but then she was on top of him, clawing at his eyes. His glasses were knocked to the floor, and he hoped fleetingly that they wouldn't be broken—

Church grabbed her somewhat brusquely by the throat and raised her off of the floor. He didn't want to hurt her, but he couldn't just *stand* there, not when there was so much to be discussed—

"Let her go, fuckhead, get down on the floor!" Crespi pointed a handgun at him, his shoulders tensed, his stance one of a man who meant business.

McGuinness struggled in his grasp like a fly on a pin, her feet still kicking wildly, but already she was starting to slow. He could feel her pulse throbbing madly beneath his fingers as she gasped vainly for air.

"Tell her to behave, Crespi." If she died, his job would be that much more difficult.

"Let her go and get down on the damn floor!"

Well, at least he hadn't called him "fuckhead" again; such *language*.

McGuinness had almost ceased to struggle, so Church dropped her, pushed her away. She was undamaged, but just lay there, breathing raggedly.

"Get on the floor! *Now!*" Crespi was still waving his weapon arrogantly.

"Don't presume to give me orders," Church said mildly.

"Get *down!*" Crespi's face had gone a dull red, and Church could see that his breaking point was close. It was time to explain, but Crespi was beyond listening, probably wouldn't hear a word as long as he held that gun ...

"That's an interesting weapon," said Church. "May I see it?"

He stepped forward and plucked the firearm from Crespi's hand, moving back before the angry doctor could register what was happening; he still stood in firing stance, incensed at Church's disobedience.

Again, those priceless faces! Anger gave way to sheer surprise, McGuinness on her knees, her expression awed and frightened. Crespi stared down at his hand, as if the weapon had simply vanished—which it had probably seemed to, to his eyes.

Church examined the machine, having to peer closely without his glasses. "Pretty little toy ... well made, too. Japanese, isn't it?"

He bent the short barrel downward, rendering the weapon useless in only a few seconds. He *was* tired; it actually took a bit of effort.

Crespi's mouth was still open. "You're—you're a synth!"

Church smiled and handed back the inert weapon, then crouched down, searching for his spectacles.

"No, not a synth. Aside from several implants, I'm quite human."

There, a meter to the left! The lenses were still intact, too. Church retrieved them, polished them quickly as he stood.

He slipped them back on, then faced Crespi; he was the one who deserved the explanation, and the one who might actually listen; the woman was hopeless, a hysteric. "You found what you were looking for, didn't you? Only you don't know what it is you've *found*—"

McGuinness crawled to her feet, crying bitterly. "Yuh-you kuh-kuh *killed* . . ."

Church shook his head. "No, I didn't kill him. I didn't kill anyone."

Crespi had dropped his toy and gone to the woman, stood now with his arm around her. They both seemed blatantly stunned at his denial, their gazes disbelieving, wary . . .

It had been a long, long time since he had told the story, decades—and even then, he'd left out bits and pieces, claiming not to remember all of it. The various military shrinks, the doctors, the Company people . . . all of them had wanted to *know*, perhaps to live the experience he'd suffered vicariously, their own foolishly pleasant lives perhaps not enough for them.

He'd revealed some of it to David, who had tried to understand, and in the end, been unable. And now again, his new assistant—for Crespi to fully comprehend his research, the story would have to be told again, maybe for the last time . . .

Church suddenly found that he *wanted* to tell it, all of it, even the parts that he had tried to forget through the years, tried and failed. He was tired of being alone, tired of the dreams and memories that he had grown accustomed to locking away, sharing with no one.

Crespi might hear him, might hear the unasked plea—and might, in some small way, relate to the experience. Total acceptance would always be beyond their grasp, but to make the attempt . . .

Why not?

Why, indeed. Crespi cleared his throat and after a moment he began to speak.

"You can't possibly be expected to understand what you see here unless you know something of my personal history—so let's have no more outbursts, and I'll tell you what happened.

"My parents' ship was the *Incunabulum*, a basic terraform spacer from forty-some years back. The crew was small, but we were carrying passengers when we set down on a numbered moon to collect a time box—there were ten of us in all. That moon is still just a number, but it's been inhabited for some time—"

He smiled vaguely, recalling his first few moments there.

Eden . . .

He shook the memory. "I hear it's quite nice, actually, although I have never been back.

"My parents and I were close, and the crew like family. I was born in space, you know, never even saw Earth until I was six; my early life was spent on ships and touring Genesis camps—an unnatural life for a young man, but I didn't mind."

Church smiled again. "It's hard to believe I was twenty. Just twenty . . ."

He closed his eyes for a moment, let the memories come flooding back, overwhelming in their sudden clarity. He was ready; it was time.

He opened his eyes. And told them everything.

20

As the drones came closer, Paul noticed that there were small, spiderlike creatures lying motionless on the floor of the cavern. They had long, spiny tails like the drones, but there the resemblance ended—

His parents crowded around him, ready to be taken first. Rebecca was crying softly, the desolate sound almost lost in the drones' hissing anticipation.

Amys Johanson was snatched up by the nearest drone. He shouted, terrified—

—as the drone extended its inner mandibles slowly and brushed the deadly apparatus against Johanson's stubbled cheek. The malignant creature hissed and dropped him roughly back to the ground.

It then reached out slowly, talons extended, and grabbed a handful of the crewman's hair. It yanked suddenly, the hair coming away in a clump. Johanson put a hand on his bleeding scalp and backed away, confusion competing with terror across his homely features.

The drone studied the uprooted handful, then dropped it, tilting its head to one side as the hair drifted to the sticky floor.

What—

Paul didn't have time to complete the thought. Another drone stepped forward and pulled him from between his clutching, wailing parents. He screamed, knew it was over, he would die first—

The drone stuck one sharp, reeking claw into his open mouth and probed at his tongue. Paul gagged and tried to back away, but the creature gripped the back of his head patiently and continued to probe.

The horrible stink of the place had almost been enough, but now Paul couldn't stop himself. He vomited, great heaves of half-digested food and bile spewing out over the drone's fingers and onto the floor.

The alien tilted its head to one side, released him— and then ran its vomit-drenched hand across its glistening teeth. It hissed and backed away.

One by one, the drones came forward, touching the humans, probing them, sniffing, pulling at clothes, their behavior unheard of by Paul or any of the others. They were being *examined* by the nightmares, and somehow it was more frightening than the prospect of death, poked and pried at by the grinning, stinking monsters in their fetid nest—

"Rebecca!"

Paul spun at the sound of Quentin Clark's shrill scream, saw him struggle desperately to free himself of a drone's tight grasp. Rebecca's mother was curled up on the floor, unconscious—

Two of the creatures had her, seemed to be fighting over her. One had her by the arms and was growling, a low, menacing rattle. The other had one of Rebecca's legs and was pulling, its desperate shrieks blending with Rebecca's, except hers were in terror—and then in pain.

Judith ran forward, her program finally activated. She jumped in between them, snatched at the pulling drone's claw—

A terrible rending sound, muscle and bone torn apart. The drones fell backward amid Rebecca's dying screams. Blood spurted from the socket of the girl's hip where her leg had been, spouted and then gushed as her cries faltered, as her heart stopped.

Everyone was screaming then, Lucien Church clutching her son, praying, sobbing, Louise awake now, she and her husband both fighting to get to their daughter.

Judith was grabbed by one of the watching drones, held—and then beaten with Rebecca's dismembered leg, pounded with the limb by the alien she had tried to stop. Judith wasn't built to withstand so much; her milky fluids splattered, mixed with the blood from Rebecca Clark's torn flesh. She crumbled, arms still flailing—until the drone that held her ripped them off and tossed them carelessly aside.

"Get back, everyone get back!" Taylor screamed and held up his fist, suddenly dark and overlarge—a grenade taken from the ship's stores. Paul watched on helplessly, sick with dread and loss as Taylor hurled himself toward the largest group of screaming drones, watched—

—until he was yanked down by his father, pulled to the bloody ground, and shielded by Jason Church's trembling body.

An explosion, his father's flinch, the blast blotting out the alien screams for only a second, Paul pleading to whatever God existed to make it count, to kill them all . . .

Church smiled sadly. "He only took out two of the drones; a token protest, really."

He shook his head, remembered the crewman's gravelly voice, his strong, blunt presence. "Taylor. God, how that man loved his cigars . . ."

A tangent. Church sighed, reluctantly let the memory go, and then went on.

"After that, they moved quickly. We were separated, and I was forced into the deepest bowels of the hive. On the way, I saw what had happened to the crew of that other ship . . ."

Paul stopped struggling when he realized that it didn't make a difference. He was using all his strength up and the drone that clutched him wasn't phased, still carried him along without effort through the dim, foul passages.

He let the drone pull him along and searched desperately for some mode of escape; if there was one, he didn't see it. The nest was solid, the dark alien secretions sturdy and seamless.

Although his nose was plugged, running with mucus from his crying, he could still smell the vile air, the rotten, decayed stink of the place—and now, as they started down another passage, some part of the rancid scent grew stronger.

Once, his family had uncovered a smuggler's body on one of their scheduled stops, a sexless, half-buried corpse that had died from a bullet in its back, undoubtedly from a greedy shipmate's gun. The smuggler had perhaps been dead for months and the stink had been awful, vicious and rank.

This new smell was similar, but multiplied a thousandfold. Paul stared around dully through tear-swollen eyes but could see no corpses, no human—

A dripping sound, overhead. Paul looked up, knowing already what he would see, trying and failing to steel himself against the sight.

There were at least a dozen human beings hung from the ceiling, their bodies naked and bloated, mouths gaping open in silent screams. Men and women, faces and limbs strung together with the alien webbing, woven into a grotesque, living tapestry of mutilation—but only partly living. The stink was from those that had died, their corpses putrefying into malodorous liquid flesh that spattered softly to the ground.

Incubators. This is what happens, what will happen to us . . .

The drone carried him past, the dangling limbs of the human incubators brushing against his hair with cold, dead fingers; he was taken to a bare place against the back wall, pushed up against it roughly. A pool of greenish-gray liquid was nearby, the opaque slime teeming with tiny tadpole creatures, but Paul didn't even hazard a guess as to what they were for; he could only stare at the hanging forest of flesh and try not to see it. He was beyond guessing, beyond anything but a dull numbness.

He was attached to the wall with thick strands of the weblike secretion, his arms strung over his head, one leg up and the other half on the ground. The drone chittered, a low clucking sound, then turned and left him there to contemplate his fate.

Hours passed, the only sound there that of the slow dripping in front of him and the occasional unconscious moan from one of the dying incubators. Hours and hours and hours. The dim light faded, went away, came back. Paul screamed for a while, then slept, then awoke to scream again, but nothing changed.

Sometimes from far away, he heard other screams, distant human voices begging and sobbing, but they never lasted very long. He wasn't sure if he cared, but thought that he had at some point before—before his eyes and nose had been scoured by the hideous stench, before that girl had been ripped to pieces. Before he was shown what he was to become . . .

When they finally appeared, he wasn't sure how he felt about it. Two dark shapes loped forward, past the hanging vines, straight at him; he eyed them suspiciously, tried to think—

They've come to kill you now.

Paul smiled, then laughed, welcoming the creatures in a voice that was high and unknown to him. He was going to die! It was . . .

He searched through the darkness of his mind for the symbols, the word that it was . . . it was—a *miracle*, that was it! He thanked them as best he could, nodding and babbling sounds that seemed familiar to some part of him. He would be free from this place, free to rest his aching eyes, to sleep and never have to dream ...

He was wrong.

"They had come to feed me," he said quietly. "One of the drones buried its face into a hanging corpse, then came to me and covered my mouth with its own, forcing the rotten flesh down my throat. They wanted me alive, at least for a while ...

"The feeding was interrupted by a scream, the worst sound I've ever heard, before or since—it was human, but only because it came from a human body; whatever had made Quentin Clark a human was irretrievably gone.

"Another drone brought him into the chamber, and he screamed on and on, blood on his lips from his shredded vocal cords; he was quite insane, you see, driven mad by whatever horrors he'd endured in that stinking hell.

"One of his arms was half gone, a scrap of cloth tied above his elbow as a makeshift tourniquet. And there was a huge, ragged hole in the crotch of his pants, the tatters remaining stained with blood and bits of flesh.

"He didn't stop screaming when they pushed him into that pool of green liquid, forcing him to drink. He continued to scream as they glued his head to the wall ... and then screamed after they left him, on and on, hour after hour, until he only made a horrible gobbling sound like a goose.

"It was about then that I started trying to swallow my own tongue ..."

Church paused, smiled wryly at the pale, mute faces of his audience.

"As you've surely guessed, I didn't succeed. I don't know why I was kept alive, or why I was separated from the others; perhaps they were also isolated and I was just the last in line for whatever they wanted us for, I honestly never understood why and probably never will ...

"I survived because I had no alternative, although for a while after that, I lost my grip on reality. I'm not sure for how long; days, I suppose. Ultimately, my mind simply retreated into itself ..."

... movement, and a sudden sharp pain, joined by another, then too many to count. He moaned, felt his body jostled roughly by bony fingers, his numb limbs abruptly alive and screaming with needles of agony.

Eyes opened from the pain. Before him, a man in a scummy pond of fluid, swollen and dead. He frowned, knew something about the man—

—*he stopped screaming, he finally stopped screaming* ...

"Clark," he rasped, but wasn't sure what that meant. The thing that held him didn't answer, but dragged him away and through an indefinite darkness.

Time and movement, and an opening of space. He was put down, landed and crumpled to a sticky floor. New place, new sounds—sucking, slurking noises. Soft wet meat noises.

Something clicked inside.

Paul raised his head wearily, blinking. He'd been dreaming for a long time, something about a ship and Quentin Clark, shouting—

Screaming, and he wouldn't stop; that wasn't a dream . . .

Consciousness, and Paul didn't like it, didn't *want* it, but he remembered everything now. He must have blacked out for a time, but the drones had come back, taken him down from the wall, taken him—

Paul looked around, saw the strange, egglike orbs all around him in the high-walled room. He crawled, stumbled to his feet, saw the lithe black figures crouching nearby, watching a struggling human figure—the person, *woman* impossibly bloated, her hands secured to the floor, her movements weak and her form wracked with pain.

He was in their breeding pen. And Louise Clark was about to give birth.

21

The drones ignored him, surrounded the moaning woman, chittered and hissed. Paul was transfixed by the sight, unable to move in his terror, and he watched helplessly as one of the drones moved closer, laid one claw gently against her monstrous, naked belly. Stroked it, pushing away the few remaining rags of her clothing to expose the stretched flesh.

I have to do something, *help her*—

He started to tremble all over, his mind screaming to turn back into its earlier void. There was nothing he could do, nothing.

A ripple of movement beneath her skin, a sliding finger beneath a flesh blanket. Louise convulsed, her back arching, her mouth screaming with no sound, nothing but the faintest gasp for air.

Her eyes opened and fixed on Paul's for one long second, the most tortured expression he'd ever seen.

She knows, Holy Mother, she knows *what's happening!*

Louise rolled her head against the ground, back and forth, the movements becoming wilder as another ripple stretched at her swollen womb. Her mouth opened again, and this time she *did* scream, one long, piercing cry of agony and awareness.

Her belly ruptured, burst outward in a spray of gore, and still she screamed, alive and *knowing*, screamed as the drone nearest reached into her throbbing gut and pulled free a tiny parasite . . .

She died with her eyes open, her purpose served for the capering monsters. They snatched up two more of the horrid things, dripping with Louise's ruptured tissues. Hissing excitedly, they held up their small, weakly squirming children, the newborn drones different than the spider creatures he'd seen before, longer, eelish—

Those dead fingered things were first stage, and then the thought that sent him over: *she had triplets . . .*

Paul vomited, not knowing that there was anything left for his body to expel. Chunks of bloody flesh spewed from his mouth, the sight and smell of it causing him to heave again.

The drones didn't seem to notice; they had begun to shriek, the sounds angry and terrible. Paul looked up, nauseous and sick and so afraid for his sanity, for his *soul*, that it took him a moment to realize what had happened.

Their babies were dying. Two of them had stopped

moving already, and in less than a minute, the third squealed faintly and joined its bloody siblings.

Dead.

The drones screeched on, the echoes in the giant chamber still furious and awful—but suddenly Paul thought that maybe their cries were *more*, they sounded—

Frustrated.

Afraid.

Something was wrong with the hive.

"From that moment forward, I kept my eyes and mind open for any information that would help me with my new resolve; I would find a way to kill them all. Some sickness had invaded their nest, they were vulnerable to it, and if I could discover the cause, could utilize it somehow . . .

"I swore then that I would survive, would make myself into the deadliest enemy the aliens had ever known. Why they had taken me to that birthing chamber, I don't know, and at the time, didn't care; all I knew was that I was still alive and that I would find a way to *stay* alive. And a way to make them sorry for not killing me first.

"When they led me away from that place, I observed. I saw things that had been there before, but in my panic had failed to notice—drones, dead and decaying. More of the tiny, spidery parasites littering the ground, stacked in piles at every corner, along with some of those eelish children like those that had come from Louise. And some of the adult creatures were slower than others, sick with whatever disease was there, their exoskeletons dull, their movements shaky.

"I was taken to a chamber where I saw what was left of Hewett and Johanson—they were beyond being able to recognize me."

Church faltered, remembered the wide, blasted eyes of the crewmen, the grasping, empty faces. He shook it off and continued.

"I was led to another of those stinking pools—but I didn't wait for the aliens to force me. With a supreme effort of will, I put my face into the murky liquid and made a show of drinking eagerly. I hoped that if I complied, I'd be spared the treatment that had made inhuman things of my crewmates.

"From the start, this plan met with success. The aliens did not molest me as long as I anticipated their actions. I—my friends were past being able to fend for themselves . . ."

Church trailed off. His audience didn't need to know how he'd fed the two dying men, carried the squirming, nameless parasites in his mouth to theirs, watched their grinning, idiot faces as they swallowed—

". . . so when I saw them doing a task I thought I could emulate, I took it upon myself; I'd do anything to prove I wasn't a troublemaker.

"Soon, the aliens stopped guarding me so closely and I was able to investigate my surroundings. I gathered as many samples of organic substances around me as I could, and kept them hidden in a small recess—I began to conduct crude experiments, testing the reactions of the samples on one another. The leechlike things in those pools, all throughout the nest—they secreted a solventlike colloid, which the aliens were evidently cultivating as a sort of medicine. And after much trial and error, I discovered that that secretion destroyed a certain ubiquitous black mold that was toxic to the drones. The drones had been trying to immunize us against whatever was making them sick, to experiment on us, I suppose, to discover a cure for their disease.

"Days, perhaps weeks, had passed, but I finally *had* something, something that the drones were incapable of understanding; I had the key to their survival in my hand.

"I immediately put my findings to use, using large quantities of the toxic mold to destroy those living medicine factories. It was amazing how well it worked; in a matter of days, drones were dying from their polluted serum. I made use of every chance I had to conduct this—biological sabotage, still searching for more, my experiments growing in range and complexity with each day.

"Thoughts of escape became secondary to the results of my work; I used my crewmates' skulls for dishes, their skin for forming vessels, arteries for tubing—any and everything I could find that would assist me in my search . . ."

Church remembered watching them, recalled the heady sense of power that had come to him with each drone falling, dying. He had been reared to believe that they were all but indomitable, almost impossible to kill—and yet there he had been, surviving among them. Poisoning them, fooling them. Learning their secrets.

And so obsessed with his experiments that he'd long stopped wondering how it would all end . . .

*   *   *

Paul shambled down the passage toward his secret cache, giggling to himself. Four more today, four! The last had died at his feet, its spiny, dusky arms wasted and reaching, its dying rattle slow, suffering . . .

Movement behind him. Paul stopped, head down, waiting for the drone to pass; they didn't see him anymore, he was just another shadow, harmless and—

A talon, cold and mute against his bony shoulder. The creature hissed dully, sickly, turned him around, and shoved him in the opposite direction, following close behind.

Another feeding. Paul frowned unhappily, hurrying ahead of the drone. It must be taking him to eat something; all of the humans were certainly dead, had been for many days. His stomach rumbled at the thought of food, accompanied closely by a roiling queasiness; the matter they fed him was too decayed to provide much nourishment anymore.

They reached an opening in the dim passage and Paul started down the left fork, where the last of the—

Amys! His name was Amys!

—food was kept. The drone screeched at him and he turned, surprised. It still stood in the open passage, waiting. He turned back, confused. There was no other way to go . . .

The creature snatched at his arm, pulled him toward a towering heap of drone corpses. It yanked him roughly around the pile, pushing at the decayed mass—

—and behind it, another passage, small and dark.

Paul smiled in spite of his uncertainty. He was being taken somewhere *new*, a place he hadn't yet visited with his poisons. Perhaps there was another pool there . . .

Or it's finally my turn to die.

He pushed the thought aside, focused on what he *could* control. The drone hissed again, and he started down the passage eagerly. It was empty, very dark, but after a moment or two he could make out a dimness ahead, another chamber.

He could hear more of the dying drones there, had come to know the sound of the disease in their cries, the reedy whistle of their breathing. There were five of them in the entry; they parted so that he could step into the small chamber.

He looked around quickly, grinning, then frowning; no pool, but a large, sloping cradlelike thing built up out of alien secretions that dominated the room, the only thing there. And inside the cradle, a human figure.

It was his mother.

Paul felt something deep inside of him shrivel and die. He had thought that there was nothing else for him to endure, no other terror that could get through to him, no atrocity left . . .

She must have fought them all along the way; her arms and legs were but rotting stumps, bitten or torn off. Her skin was covered with dozens, hundreds of lacerations, claw marks—

Impossibly, horribly, she lived. He could hear her unconscious breathing, shallow and slow, each intake of foul air stabbing at the remnants of his soul . . .

A drone shoved him rudely forward; he barely stopped before he would have fallen in, landed on top of her—

"Nooo—" he moaned, felt his sanity curdle, prepared to depart forever as he realized why he'd been brought to this place.

The creatures wanted them to mate. To make healthy, new incubators.

Paul felt the chamber spinning, darkness clouding his vision, and he knew he wouldn't be able to keep his awareness for much longer, couldn't stop himself from falling into the void. He bent over her, the drones leaning in, hissing gleefully—

Paul remembered her smile, her laugh, the way she'd had of touching her hair when she was nervous—all of that gone, ripped away . . .

He gently, tenderly wrapped his trembling hands around his mother's fevered throat and did the only thing he could to ease her suffering.

One of the drones shrieked, grabbed for him, but it was weak from the sickness—and too late. Lucian's eyes bulged open in the last seconds of her life, strangled by her only son, and he saw the pain there, the insanity—

And the final, small flicker of gratitude. He wept, calling her name as the room spun faster, as the drones snatched him away from her mutilated corpse . . .

. . . a

. . . everything went to black.

"When I awoke again, I was secured to one wall of their breeding pen. The aliens gave their best shot; their last chance, really . . .

"They brought an egg, opened it in my face. The sickness had affected even those; they had to help the weak face-hugger out of its shell. Still, it was stronger than I.

"It forced my lips and jaws apart ... shoved its probe down my trachea. And into my chest."

Church stopped for a moment, found that he couldn't go on, not yet. He could almost *feel* it, as he sometimes did in his dreams—the prehensile coiled tail, closing around his throat, tightening ...

He looked up, saw Crespi and McGuinness there, waiting, their expressions unreadable. Finally, Crespi broke the silence, his voice soft and somehow bland.

"But ... how? How did you survive?"

Church smiled faintly. "Who says I did?"

22

Church studied their faces, read the mute shock there, and decided to finish his little tale; there was still much to do, and the emotions he had stirred within himself weren't what he had expected, not at all. He'd hoped for a catharsis, an understanding—and what he felt was . . . unclear.

Later; that will have to suffice for now.

"I suppose I thought that I had at last been killed, but that merciful oblivion ended. I awoke, and I was alone. I could feel the heavy parasitic load cradled in my chest; it was . . . *obscene*, that feeling, that sick, leaden weight. There's no way to describe it, feeling that and knowing what it meant for me.

"The aliens' secretions had weakened with their sickness; I pulled free easily, and none of the creatures came to stop me. The smell of death was everywhere, the aliens, the crew . . .

—*the dark, murky stench, the stumbling footsteps to get away, the madness dulled by days of terror and that final act*—

"I didn't look for my father; I didn't want to see what they'd done to him. All I wanted was to die, but not inside the hive.

"The passage to the outside was unguarded, and I realized then that they were all dead. Still, I expected to be stopped somehow; I didn't think it was possible that I would be allowed to just *leave*, to walk out as if none of that nightmare had ever occurred . . . but I did. Walked out into the open space, walked away from that dead hive and into the light; the place that had once seemed an Eden to me was no longer.

"The fresh air, the brightness, they were quite a shock to my ravaged senses. I collapsed just outside the nest, but I was happy, knew then that I would at least die with the sun on my face.

"After a time, I found I could go on. I passed the smugglers' ship and returned to the *Incunabulum*. It was untouched, humming, power levels full.

"This then was my homecoming. Our comfortable ship, sweet and dependable, full of warm ghosts that loved me. I saw by the terrestrial calendar that I had been in the hive for forty-three days; not such an eternity as I'd dreamed . . .

"I thought of my family and those aliens lying dead together, almost in each other's arms. In death, they were united; I alone had emerged from that apocalypse. I was alive, but I can't say that I had *survived;* the Paul Church that had been was no longer. And perhaps . . . perhaps for a *reason.*

"Suddenly, I wanted—I was desperate to live, to start over. I didn't question it as I didn't question why I alone had made it out alive—but I can tell you that the feeling was overwhelming and beautiful, like a cold splash of water on dehydrated flesh. Not to waste my rebirth, squander it away in selfishness, but to go on, to keep searching for a solution. So I sent a distress signal.

"It took me four hours to cleanse my body. I patched my wounds, then used the ship's ultrasound to examine the alien larva in my chest. It was dead, dead and rotting; its immediate removal was imperative.

"I had no surgical experience at all, but I gathered what information and tools I could and set to work. The ship had a fairly extensive medical center, thankfully. The operation took seven hours, but it was a complete success.

"When the rescue party arrived a month later, I met them on my own two feet—though I was an atrophied mess by then, alive but in poor condition.

"I was debriefed at length. It turned out that the smugglers—aspiring bug farmers, if you can believe it—were responsible for the hive.

"The Company considered my experience most valuable. As compensation for my ordeal in the service of the government, I was granted a full biomechanical makeover. The hive was destroyed before I had a chance to tell them about that toxic mold or the colloid leeches, most unfortunate for all of us; I've tried to replicate some version of the mold many times—unsuccessfully so far—and I've never heard of any species like those swimming parasites. But I've been studying aliens ever since. And someday . . ."

Church sighed, then motioned around him in a sweeping gesture. "There are no laws that govern my research aboard this station. My work is blasphemous—abominable—*illegal*, I'm sure. And I haven't yet created an end to the alien threat. But my experiments *have* yielded some unexpected, miraculous results."

He sought out Crespi's intent gaze. "You've heard rumors, no doubt—numerous metabiotics, self-replicating brain tissue, acquired intrasensory abilities, the so-called 'time serum' . . ."

Crespi's dark eyes sharpened. "The time serum? Your work?"

"Yes. The results will benefit—"

"*Results?!*" McGuinness stepped toward him angrily, cutting him off. "You killed these people for—*science?!*"

Church met her gaze dead-on. "I've killed no one. I appropriated the bodies of soldiers who died in the line of duty. The chemicals that their bodies put out are invaluable; they're the key to the final solution—the scarring, the mutations, are necessary, if distasteful. Each reaction is carefully measured and recorded, and the results are used in the creation of new telepathine drugs—synthesized chemicals that will bring an eventual end to the alien threat.

"And you accuse me of murder? Really, McGuinness, you already know the truth. Stop playing innocent."

She looked to Crespi, suddenly confused. And quite anxious.

"I have no idea what he—"

Church frowned. "Oh, please. You're not the only

one handy with spy cameras; you showed Crespi a doctored photo that convinced him that you and David Lennox were engaged."

She was openly shocked now. "What—?"

Church looked sadly at the man-computer that had once been his assistant. "David was a body donor; he believed in me. You hardly knew him at all . . ."

Church turned back to them. McGuinness stuttered, incensed and still disbelieving.

"You—you *liar*—"

Church shook his head sadly, looked back at David. "I should know. David and I were lovers."

"*No!* He's *lying*, Crespi, don't listen to him!"

Church spun back, addressed Crespi firmly. "Think about it, and think well, Crespi! Mortenson was a spy for Grant Corporation; Admiral Thaves *knew*, he pegged him! Mortenson was under constant surveillance by ship's orders, but he ditched us somehow, ended up dead . . . and Sharon McGuinness was his partner."

She shifted her panicked gaze between the two men. "It's a lie!"

Church glared at her. "That'll be for a tribunal to decide. Now, Colonel Doctor, if you'll be so kind as to arrest this woman—"

"Crespi—Tony, *please!* He'll kill me!"

Crespi wavered, looked at Church and then the woman, his face undecided. If Crespi was reasonable, *logical*, he would see the truth of what Church said, would have no other choice. Church waited, wondered what he would do—if he was as bright as he seemed to be.

McGuinness stood with her back to the partly

opened hatch; if Crespi made the right decision, would she run?

So many unanswered questions . . .

The three of them stood there silently, a triangle of hope and despair and truth, waiting, locked in place for the decision to come.

23

Crespi had listened to the doctor's story, fascinated, sickened, and finally in awe of Paul Church. A lesser man would not have survived, let alone flourished as Church had done. This man had *lived* among the loathsome breed, exploited and then killed them with little more than his mind and bare hands ...

And now this—accusation. It was almost too much for his fuzzy, exhausted mind to grasp. He stared at Church, thought about what he'd said, saw the clear, steady gaze, confident and certain. If he was lying, he was doing it very well.

He looked to McGuinness, the woman he thought he knew. Her eyes were wide and frightened, pleading. She'd played it straight with him, hadn't she? The code slate *had* been the key to the hidden lab, she'd gotten him in, had been as shocked and horrified as he was.

Except—did that make her innocent?

There were holes in her story, perhaps—holes in Church's, too, but it all came down to who he believed, her word against his. If she had lied to him about how many crew fatalities there had been and she *could* have, could have lied about everything—

And Mortenson. What *had* he been doing messing around with those suits? McGuinness said station's orders, but again, her word against Church's ...

He looked back at the doctor, considered what he knew so far. Church's biomake meant that he could easily kill both of them, probably without breathing hard. Why would he lie to see McGuinness arrested if he wanted her dead, or wanted them both dead? He had admitted to everything, admitted that his work was brutal, unappealing, even illegal. And yet he sought no approval, made no excuses for what he had done.

But what about the alien in his unity lab? Who else could have let it in?

And, on the tail of that: *How could McGuinness have known about the slate and not about the drone?*

Crespi closed his eyes, tormented by conflicting emotions, truth or lie, him or her. There could be no compromise. He searched for his instincts and again couldn't find them; he was tired, so very tired, wanted only for this to be over with, just to go lay down somewhere and sleep ...

"I ... I'm sorry," he whispered.

The decision was made.

*　　　*　　　*

McGuinness was furious at the accusation, furious and desperately afraid that Crespi would listen to Church. Why was he waiting? Why was he struggling with Church's *lies*?

"I . . . I'm sorry," Crespi whispered, and when he opened his eyes, he looked at her.

"Very sorry, but I—McGuinness, I'll have to—"

She backed away, felt her arm brush against the cool metal of the hatch behind her, glanced. It opened into a long, dim corridor.

"You *monsters*," she breathed, stunned tears of disbelief welling up. *This can't be happening, can't—*

She turned and ran.

Crespi grabbed for her, but she was gone, footsteps clattering hollow down the smooth metal passage.

"McGuinness!"

He shot a look back at Church, saw the doctor move quickly to a circuit panel set in the wall.

"After her! I can control every door in the station from here, we can corner her in the pit!"

Crespi was already running, his own boots ringing down the corridor, echoing back to taunt him—

Church was right, God I've been such a fool—

This was a bad dream happening too fast—he felt as if he'd boarded a runaway rail, his car bulleting away from the sane, the rational, his intuition so muddled that he had to rely on guilty action to see him through . . .

He reached the end of the passage, turned, saw a glimpse as she ducked around the corner, still running. There were several dull *clangs* as doors closed elsewhere, limiting her escape, sealing her in.

"Give it up, McGuinness!" His shout reverberated throughout the hall, surely reached her, but still she ran.

Another bend, another flash of flying movement ahead, but he was closer, gaining. His feet pounded, angry—*Why did she have to lie, why, how could I have been so blind*—and he turned the corner, right on top of her.

She let out a moan when she saw how close he'd come, leapt forward in a burst of anxious speed. He could hear her breathing now, hear her curses.

"Stupid, stupid—" Her voice trailing behind her, turning another bend.

He ran, ducked—and she was cornered, nowhere left to run, her back against the enclosure wall, her face openly terrified—

"No!" she shouted, but she was looking *behind* him, back the way they'd come.

Crespi turned as the door to the pen slammed down, the metallic sound quiet after the bounding echoes of the passageway. He turned back, sweating, pleased; she was caught, no way for her to get away—

The look of pure panic across her features gave him pause.

"I'm not going to *hurt* you," he said, somehow hurt himself that she could think that, but she didn't seem to hear him at all.

"He's got us," she whispered, and Crespi's heart suddenly pounded even harder than when he'd run, followed by a slow, horrible sinking in his gut.

She looked up and he followed her gaze, saw Paul Church step to the railing above the kennel and call down to them.

"You really should have listened to her, Crespi."

Their captor smiled and folded his arms.

Crespi fell back against the wall, his ears hammering with dull pulses of blood, felt angry and hurt and lost all at once.

He'd made the wrong choice, and it was going to cost them.

24

hurch stood there, smiling. Crespi *was* a reasonable man; Church's story had made good, solid sense, could very well have been the truth—except it wasn't, and Crespi was apparently not so bright after all. He needed more in an assistant.

He looked down at the pair, savoring the moment. The woman had helped greatly, her panicked looks, the vehement; shouted denials—and she had run, exactly as he'd assumed she would.

Well, hoped *she would* . . .

Never mind. In the end, she'd done what he wanted, forced into play by her valiant, stupid knight.

Of course, he could have just as easily taken them here—but where was the fun in that? No, much better that Crespi had made the decision, now lived with the knowledge that he'd forsaken both himself and McGuinness, all in the name of duty . . .

Crespi made a great show of his amazement, his face red and spluttering.

"Church! What the devil are you *doing*?"

Church shook his head sadly. "Please. You flatter yourself by being surprised at how easily you've been deceived. You people can be bought with a cookie, fooled with three words—really, I can't believe how quick you were to sell out the truth for something that sounded better."

Crespi had no response, though he glanced at McGuinness somewhat guiltily.

Charming! He's gone and piddled on her carpet, feels just awful about it—"Here, my dearest, roses for you, so sorry about the mess, can you forgive me?"

Church cackled, but inside he felt something harden. It was sad, really. Pathetic.

"You're a slave to your empirical truth," he sneered. "A slave to sweetness and light. And what are they? Prosthetic abstractions conceived by embryonic minds, unable to cope with the truth! Where does good exist? Only in your empty skulls; God, if you only knew how I see you . . . *humans*."

Confusion from the little man. "But *you're* hu—"

Church sighed. "Oh, do shut up, Crespi. Must you always believe in appearances? I told you the truth already, but you didn't listen; I didn't survive the hive—I *am* the hive. When I look the cosmos in the eye, it blinks. But *you*—the good soldier, so proud of your brains, your courage—you're nothing but a fatuous rah-rah boy, so limited, so *confined*, scampering around with your tiny goals, your tiny thoughts— you're beneath my contempt, can't you see that? No better than Mortenson, or any of the others; just another warm body."

He was honestly angry, though not surprised by it. He'd had such *hope* for Crespi, had actually thought at one point that he was on the verge of understanding—of escaping the boundaries of his preconditioned, petty morality and moving beyond . . .

It hurt to be wrong. And pain always brought anger, didn't it? Next time, he'd try to keep his expectations to a minimum.

The same thing you said after David, Doctor. Really, you should try to learn from your mistakes . . .

He felt his anger dwindle and fade. Truly, it wasn't Crespi's fault that he had been overestimated, nor was he to blame for not trusting in McGuinness; humans had a nasty habit of letting each other down—dying in their quiet lack of purpose, justifying their existence with self-righteous, selfish attacks on their fellow man—

In a way, this was the best thing he could do for them, do *by* them; at least this way, their lives wouldn't be entirely useless. There was hope for Crespi yet.

Church reached down and picked up the handheld control for the electric shock device installed in the pen.

"You have the honor of contributing to my research, my *real* research—what you found back in that lab, but were too narrow-minded to see. Although you won't be in any condition to appreciate it, you will have assisted in the creation of an evolutionary bridge to the true crown of creation. The pink poetry of man will be subsumed by the black, blank genius

of the alien—and the result will be the original and final creature. It will feed and live off of itself.

"And I will join it."

He could almost feel his eyes ablaze with his inner
fire, the quest revealed at last. He felt powerful,
untouchable—

—*and to these little people, you're just chewing at
scenery; get on with it.*

He smiled to himself. There was no need to explain
any further, they would be too closed off in themselves to hear Truth—and they wouldn't understand
anyway. David hadn't, and he'd been brighter than the
two of them combined.

Church pointed at the door that would lead them
through the labyrinth. "Go through the door, both of
you."

Crespi stared up at him, almost expressionless, but
when he spoke, his voice seethed with pure, bare hatred. "Go to hell!"

"Been there," Church said mildly, and stroked the
control in his hand.

An electric pulse, sparks flying white and blue as
they both convulsed, dropped to the floor, writhed in
agony. A strange, twitching moan erupted from
Crespi, closest to the circuit, his cry low, pained.
McGuinness tried to scream "stop," stuttered and faltered, her mouth open, teeth almost *glowing*—

Church released the switch reluctantly. Too much
would kill them before they'd even had a chance to
begin—and he wanted very much to see how far they
would get before he could salvage their bodies and
examine the brain tissue for future application. The
telepathine ploy had served its purpose well, but the
chemicals he truly needed were quite different. Some

of the mutilations to his test subjects *had* been necessary in the beginning—

A fleeting thought, gone before he realized he'd had
it—

(not anymore, now you just like it)

—Church shook his head. The genetic work was
his current focus, though he still needed to do more
chemical work. To merge man and drone was no
small task, and he needed to find the common denom-
inators, the shared transmitters of rage.

Of course for it to be of any value, they had to get
started. In another hour his lab techs would be
pounding on the door . . .

"Where's your sense of sport? Make it through the
labyrinth and I might even let you live."

It sounded false even to him, but he had to give
them *some* incentive.

McGuinness crawled to the fallen doctor, slowly
righted herself, and then helped him to his feet.

"You all right?"

He coughed, shook his head. "No."

McGuinness took one of his arms and they started
for the door; wonderful! Church pressed the entry
switch, calling out after them helpfully as they entered the dark passage.

"Watch that first step, it's a lulu!"

He pressed again, sealing them into the maze, then
hurried back down the ramp to the video monitors.

The large screen flickered on, showed the two of
them standing just inside the entry, talking softly.

"Now I'm *really* sorry, McGuinness."

She smiled somewhat ironically, the camera angle
perfect. "Begging your pardon, but it's a little late for
that."

Gallows humor, how admirable! Church tapped a button, spoke into the com.

"Move along now, children, or I'll fry you where you stand."

They hesitated only a second before walking on, eyes wide in the mute darkness.

Church sat down and leaned back, smiling.

He was going to enjoy this.

25

It was dark in the passage, dark and cold. McGuinness shivered, bumps raising on the flesh of her bare arms, and wished vainly that the weather was all they had to worry about.

They moved slowly toward a closed door at the end of the corridor, the only place *to* go; she could see the tiny, steady red lights of the video cameras that lined the walls, counted them absently. Four in the short hall, four different angles so that Church would be sure to get the cleanest shot.

"Mad fucking scientist," she muttered, hoped that the audio sensors carried *that* cleanly enough. Bad enough they were being sent to almost certain death—but that it was for that sick bastard's *amusement* ...

Crespi glanced at her, then refocused his steady

gaze on the closed door. "I—shouldn't have listened to him, McGuinness; this is my fault, and—"

"No, it's his; he's doing this. He would've picked us up and carried us here if you'd decided he was lying; he's strong enough—he just wanted to watch you fuck up."

Crespi nodded, voice low. "Yeah, but I *did* fuck up—"

"I'll give you that," she whispered. "But then, I signed up for this, remember? Tell you what—why don't we get out of here and hash it out later over coffee . . ."

He nodded again, the tiniest hint of a smile on his otherwise stern face. They inched closer to the door.

It slid open suddenly in a faint hydraulic hiss. McGuinness tensed, saw Crespi do the same. They stood for a good half minute, searching the new darkness for some hint of motion, but there was nothing.

She felt some tension drain from her aching muscles, the back of her neck—but not much. The shock that Church had delivered had left her worn out and sore all over, but the adrenaline that was now surging through her system wouldn't allow her to relax, not for a second.

Good.

Crespi moved first, his expression suddenly cold and determined. A deep breath, and McGuinness followed.

Crespi tensed as the door hissed open, but there was no movement, no sudden, hurtling rush of teeth and claws. The blackness yawned before them, seemingly empty, the steady lights of the cameras ahead

providing the barest illumination; Church must be
using infra, or maybe a standard tachspeed . . .

His mind was wandering. He shook himself mentally, tried to snap out of the aching malaise that enveloped him; his senses were dulled, no sleep, the
electric shock, all that had happened so far—

If he didn't stay focused, they were dead.

*You're dead anyway, you know it. You think
Church is actually going to let you go, you really are
asleep and dreaming.*

Right. But giving up wasn't an option; he had
McGuinness to think about—

The thought stopped him. He searched the darkness ahead, frowning, replaying it again.

If it *was* just him . . .

You'd find a way to end it, wouldn't you?

No!

Maybe . . .

The inner debate was useless, moot; it wasn't just
him. But that he was that ready to die, to call an end
to Church's little game by sacrificing himself—that
was frightening, perhaps scarier than the empty
blackness in front of them and the threat of what lay
beyond . . .

*Is it? You're already dead, you died on that rock a
million years ago, when you were the only one who
walked away . . .*

Crespi scowled, suddenly furious with himself,
with his stupid, childish neuroses, the fear that he'd
carried with him for so long—and in that second, he
felt a sudden clarity, a—*letting go*, like a locked door
inside was opened, the ghosts nestled there set free.

He was alive and the enemy was near; the past
wasn't relevant. If that made him a rah-rah boy, so be

it, but he wasn't going to torment himself with his right to suck air for one more goddamn *minute*.

He stalked forward feeling suddenly wide awake, McGuinness right behind.

And stepped right into the grinning face of an alien drone, waking it up.

The creature screamed, reached for him, saliva dripping from its clutching teeth.

Crespi stumbled backward, into McGuinness, turned to run back into the empty passage behind—

"The door, don't—" McGuinness shouted, clear and terrified, and she shoved him, pushed him away from the hydraulic exit as it sealed closed, locking them in with the shrieking demon.

Crespi spun again, formed his hands into claws, ready to die fighting—

The drone struggled, its howl lowering to a hiss, talons still outstretched—but it came no closer.

It was harnessed to the wall on the left, a metal brace around its torso hooked to a reinforced panel. Its tail slapped uselessly against the floor, curling just out of reach. Enraged and helpless.

—sound familiar?

"It can't get to us," said Crespi, as much to reassure himself as McGuinness, who could surely see.

"Until Church wants it to," she said, her voice low and trembling.

His hatred for Church was complete as he searched the darkness for an escape, a way to get past the leashed creature before the deranged scientist could release it.

Church had better pray that they never got out.

*   *   *

The drone on the monitor snarled and hissed, starving, desperate to reach the captive morsels as they fell backward. Crespi would have been cut in half by the closing door if McGuinness hadn't prevented it; she was sharp, perhaps sharper than he'd first thought.

The harnessed creature moaned in hunger.

There, there, pet; doggie want a cookie?

Church let his hand hover over the release switch, then decided against it. Their adrenaline would be high, but he was hoping they would reach greater endorphin levels if let go a little longer; he needed their fury. Crespi was tired, probably the woman, too, but their anger at him would certainly blossom into some very nice testoterone . . .

"It can't get to us," said Crespi.

Oh, bravo! He's an astute one—

"Until Church wants it to." McGuinness, sounding frightened and wary.

That's right, his mind whispered, *you've hit on a great truth, madam.* Her tune was quite different than a moment or so earlier, when she'd cursed him, called him a—

Church smiled. Perhaps he should get a plaque made up of it, that would look fine on his desk: Colonel Doctor Paul Church, Mad Fucking Scientist. His associates would find it charming—

She knew who was in control here, who had the say over their survival. Did Crespi? Or did he still think that he would *win* somehow, as infantile as the concept was?

He empathized, on some level, could comprehend helpless frustration and the drive to live; they were the same as the aliens in many regards. He could even feel sorry for them, their hopes and dreams laid to rest at the touch of a button. But he had seen the Truth through countless years of observation; he knew more than they were capable of knowing. The final outcome needed to be, *would* be the ultimate achievement, the glorious end to these unfortunate means. He was not an egomaniac searching for godhood; he was—

Why, a mad fucking scientist!

Church laughed. As fitting a title as any.

He peered at the monitor, tapped a button to change shots. Crespi had spotted the ladder to the next level of the maze, the next step in their crucible.

Church grinned, tapped another button. It was time for Crespi to learn who was in charge here.

26

Crespi pointed to the farthest corner of the sealed tunnel, his hand a vague, pale shape in the darkness. "Over there!"

McGuinness looked, could see nothing except shadows, littered with camera lights. After a moment she made out a faint glow from just above where he'd pointed. And rungs, bolted into the wall.

Together, they backed to the wall opposite the clawing drone, inched closer to the ladder, just out of the creature's grasping reach. McGuinness struggled to keep her panic down, tried not to think about what Church could do with one finger, one switch to the harness release . . .

They made it past, the drone screaming almost hysterically. It was probably starving, rabid to get loose, to tear into fresh meat—

She buried the thought quickly. To their left, she could now make out another door, sealed. Up was the only way.

Crespi kept his eye on the frantic drone, motioned for her to go first. McGuinness grabbed the highest rung she could manage and started to climb.

Up and slowly up, the ladder seemed eternal, the faint light she'd noticed only a shade brighter. She was glad to be away from that hissing, shrieking darkness, but at least the drone there had been harnessed; she could be climbing into a crouching nest of them, waiting, drooling—

A sudden stab of memory from her childhood— hide-and-seek with some forgotten playmate in an abandoned house, she the seeker; at each corner, seething with unknown shadow, a deep breath, heart pounding, the knowledge strong in her young mind that any second would come the surprise—

"See anything?" His shout was hoarse and not as far below her as she'd imagined, maybe ten meters.

She looked up, checked her progress for the billionth time. The ceiling of blackness was still just overhead.

"It's too dark."

Quiet below, the drone gone back to its low hissing. Another step. Another, her hands clammy with sweat. Another.

She glanced up again. The source of light was definitely closer now; she could see where the rungs ended, an opening not far away.

A way out.

Thank God, thank God!

She called down to him excitedly. "I think I see something! There's light, it's—"

A sudden shadow, and she jerked her head up, *knew* that the hidden threat had made its move—

The alien screamed in her face, a glob of spittle smacked her chin, its claws darted forward.

And grabbed her.

Crespi heard it, heard her scream in response. He jumped to the rungs, scrambled up after her.

"Sharon!"

"Go back! Go back!"

He looked up, saw that it had a hold of her by one shoulder. Her grip on the ladder was gone, and she kicked frantically in the air, trying to get loose—

A sound like ripping cloth and she dropped a half meter, the drone screaming wildly. She hung by just her overshirt now—

—*why didn't it pull her up*—

—the material giving rapidly.

Crespi dropped back to the floor, readied to catch her, at least ease the impact—

Another scream, much closer. He spun, frantic, as a small, dim light glowed to life in the chamber, illuminating the harnessed drone.

And a click, somehow audible amid the screams, somehow incredibly loud as he realized what it meant.

Church had unleashed the alien.

McGuinness screamed for Crespi to go back. If the alien let go, she'd knock him off the ladder.

The pain was sharp, the dirty claws of the alien's

hand dug deeply into the flesh of her left shoulder. It chittered madly, tried to lift her—

And couldn't. She felt the tremble of its weakened body, realized that it wasn't strong enough.

McGuinness began to flail, kicking, tried to bounce loose. She felt her flesh give way first, long tears in her shoulder as the creature's grasp was jolted free. It clutched, shrieking—

—and she fell, but it still had her, its long fingers enmeshed in the strap of her overshirt.

The harnessed drone below seemed to scream in response, and a sudden dull light filtered up to her. She saw the blood running across her skin, soaking the tattered cloth, warming her breast.

"Let—*go*!" A final, bouncing jump and the shirt gave, the drone howling furiously as she fell, curled her arms over her head.

—*bendyourknees*—

She hit the floor, hard, felt one ankle give, pain shooting through her lower leg—but she had landed in a half crouch, and found she could stand . . .

Looked around, the corridor almost brilliantly lit after the dark climb, saw Crespi. And in front of him, the drone. Loose.

She ignored the pain, limped quickly to his side. There was nowhere else to go.

The drone was bent down, hissing, but not moving any closer.

"Church's conditioning," Crespi whispered tightly, and it clicked. The experiments had weakened them, it was why the drone at the ladder couldn't lift her. And this one was waiting, knew that it would be shocked before it could attack, was looking for the fastest way to get to them—

They had a chance.

Behind her and above she heard the hissing of the thwarted drone, descending the metal rungs or maybe just preparing to leap . . .

Movement behind her. She turned, panicked, heard the quieter hiss—

—as the door slid open, revealing another dark chamber.

"The door!"

Crespi turned, saw the opening, didn't hesitate. He grabbed her, twisted, and pushed as hard as he could. *"Move!"*

She flew, stumbling, into the corridor, landed on the floor. She jumped to her feet and turned.

The harnessed drone was joined by the other, the two of them about to lunge for Crespi, for the door—

He ran, leapt as the entry started to slide closed, fell through the narrowing gap, the creatures right behind.

She saw, could do nothing to stop it. One black talon darted forward, hit Crespi solidly, raked down—

—and then was gone, the chamber sealed.

There was blood everywhere.

27

Church frowned as Crespi crashed through the door, fell, his back ripped to pieces. It was too soon, really, although he supposed it couldn't be helped . . .

If he was dead, Church didn't want to release another drone; there'd be nothing to salvage, not as hungry as they were.

He watched as McGuinness ran to his side, watched and waited.

"Crespi? Tony?"

She crouched down, a tight glance around the newest corridor, no drones, back to him, feeling sick and afraid, feeling like her earlier terror was nothing to what she experienced now.

Crespi lay facedown, unmoving, the back of his shirt bloodied and shredded from the shoulders down to the bottom of his spine.

—please don't let him die, don't leave me alone here—

She pulled off the last of her tattered sleeveless overshirt, folded it, and looked for a place to staunch the blood flow. There was so *much*, it was impossible to tell where the worst was, where to put the compress—

He moaned, stirred, then winced in pain.

"You're hurt, shh, lay still," she said, and placed one hand against the back of his head, stroked the dark, short hair there, feeling desperately frightened and not knowing what to do anymore.

He's going to die, *soldier, you both are if you don't keep moving!*

She knew it, but couldn't make herself stand, wouldn't.

She wouldn't leave him to die alone.

Crespi's back was on fire. He groaned, tried to move—

God! The pain was incredible, all-consuming, as if someone had whipped him mercilessly, flayed the living flesh until it had separated from the bone. Wet, thick heat spilled across his wounds, and he knew it was bad, really bad.

McGuinness was near, telling him to lie still in a low, trembling voice, gently touching his hair. He kept his eyes closed, tried to concentrate on the feel of her hand; a woman's hand, it brought up memories from before he was aware—a crooning, soft lullaby, the stroke of warm fingers . . .

It was impossible. He was going to die, bleed to death on the dark floor of Church's dark labyrinth. If the drones didn't come first and rip them apart.

Church.

From out of his pain, he found focus. The man who'd done this to him, a sociopath who had kept his dark side hidden and hidden well, who had lied to his face and then sent him to death—all for the sake of his twisted, blasphemous work. The man who would kill Sharon McGuinness next, this good woman who waited to die beside him.

Paul Church.

Suddenly he was filled with a new heat, and it overrode his pain, beat it out in its raw, burning intensity. He opened his eyes, saw the shadowed chamber through a veil of red.

Slowly, incredibly, he pushed himself up, felt the strain in his battered flesh, felt the wounds in his back scream anew as fresh blood poured over them.

He started to stand, almost didn't make it, but McGuinness was there, supporting him. He saw that she was injured, too, the skin of her shoulder ripped, the blood spilled out and drying on her tight undershirt.

"You—shouldn't have changed on my account," he said, but it came out in a rough whisper, hoarse.

"Tony—" Her voice said most of it, her expression the rest: concern, fear, confusion, and pain.

He managed a smile as best he could. "I'm—I'm fine. And I'm going to get us out of here."

They started through the dim hall, and Crespi

started to look for a way to end it; Church was a dead
man.

Church grinned, silently applauding Crespi's struggle. Such determination! It was amazing, how one
could still hope, even knowing that hope was all they
had . . .

He frowned, remembering all too well how hard
that could be.

Dark, reeking tunnels, dark paths, dark mind,
"Paul—" his mother's scream and hope, only hope—
. . . the scalpel enters cold flesh . . .

Suddenly he didn't feel like playing anymore. He
sighed, disappointed that it would be cut short, but it
was best. Like it or not, part of him was still human,
could still relate to some of the display; it was a
weakness, to be sure, but he could not deny it.

It was over.

"Good-bye, Doctor Crespi. Good-bye, McGuinness.
It's been—interesting."

With that, he punched the button to release the final drone.

Crespi seemed to be looking for something, his
pained gaze searching the dark walls as they stumbled
slowly down the sealed corridor.

She was stunned and relieved that he could still
function, could still move at all—but it couldn't last
long, whatever was driving him to continue; his back
was torn open, the muscles clawed to tatters. A slick
trail of blood followed them, pattering thickly, the
back of his pants soaked with it.

This part of the labyrinth had no exit, it seemed, the door at the opposite end sealed. It was lit darkly from another opening overhead, at least a meter beyond their reach, the light murky and shadowed.

With a low grunt, Crespi started to kick at the wall, at the bolted electrical shock circuit. It was a small device, a little bigger than her fist perhaps, and torn from the cords it was useless as a weapon—

"Help me," he breathed, and stopped, his breath low and ragged, his waxen forehead beaded with sweat.

She kicked at it, hitting at the supporting metal bar with the heel of her boot. They alternated, both of them sweating now, grunting with exertion.

Crespi was kicking hard, his face livid now, beating at the straining metal with almost superhuman strength. He started to mutter, spitting out words with each impossible kick.

"Church—wants to—show *us*, I'll—show—*him*!"

With a final rending *crack* the support bar clattered to the ground, the metal bent away at one of the heavy screws. The electrical cord was still tacked to the wall, but it hissed angrily at them, spit out tiny blue sparks from the small break they'd caused.

Crespi bent with a cry of triumph and pain, scooped up the thick, heavy bar. It was maybe the length of his forearm, each end bent slightly where it had been bolted to the circuit panel.

"I'm going to kill him," Crespi said, and he meant it, heart and soul; his eyes were black, focused in hate, his mouth an angry white line.

McGuinness nodded, knew that's what carried him now. He was sure as hell going to *try*, she could see that. Watching his eyes, she hoped to God that she didn't happen to get in the way; he was in bad shape, but so concentrated in his fury that he didn't seem to notice anymore.

She looked back at the sealed door behind them, then to the one ahead. "Where to now?"

Crespi started to respond, but she never found out what he meant to suggest. From overhead, a shriek, the running clatter of a drone's movement, close.

Crespi raised the metal bar, faced the hole in the ceiling. "Get back," he said, his voice commanding, powerful.

The clattering, heavy steps louder now. A shadow fell across the opening, blotting out the already dim light.

A strange chittering sound, then an expectant, greedy hiss.

It dropped down into the corridor ready to attack, its body tensed in a crouch, about to pounce—

And Crespi stepped in to meet it, eyes burning.

He swung the bar, a cry of pure rage erupting from his throat, aimed for the drone's gleaming, slick head, his whole body following through—

SMACK, the metal connected solidly, cracked against the long skull with a wet sound, its blood spewing—

"*No!*" McGuinness stumbled back, screaming!

The door at the end of the hall slid open as the drone shrieked, a bubbling, thick sound, its fluids a sizzling gush, poured across the metal bar, the walls—

And onto Crespi.

Incredibly, the drone turned and ran through the open door.

Crespi crumpled to the floor.

*   *   *

Crespi felt the alien acid hit him, the thick, viscous gush land against his chest in a dull splash as McGuinness screamed.

—not like this—

His last truly coherent thought before his clothes were eaten away, the acid burning into his flesh, branding him with white-hot intensity.

He fell, his knees giving way beneath the incredible burning agony, landed on his back, and *could not* scream, the pain blinding, his fingers curled, knotted in front of him.

—dead I'm notdeadyet—Church—

Somewhere, he found the strength; he opened his mouth and screamed, a horrible, frustrated cry, all of his anger and pain combined, poured his very soul into the long, terrible sound.

He was dying, and Church was still alive.

He had failed.

McGuinness covered her face with her hands at Crespi's tortured cry, the tears springing unbidden to her eyes. Such torment in that awful sound, such bleak despair.

She stumbled to him, careful even in her grief to avoid the hissing splatters of acid, knelt beside him.

He was still alive. Church's experiments must have done something to their defense mechanisms, weakened their blood—

She hoped blindly, for one agonizing second, that he could survive, could be saved.

It's not as bad as it looks, can't *be, he can make it—*

She lifted his head gently, rested it against one

shaking leg, looked down at his chest and abdomen—and then quickly looked away. The front of his torso was a smoking puddle, a frothy mass of blood and disintegrating bone.

She reached for his hand, felt his fingers weakly curl around hers. He was barely conscious; she saw sickly that each breath bubbled in his gut, and when he opened his mouth, blood poured out over his pale lips, reddening them.

He rolled his eyes, gazed up at her glassily, as if he saw something else, some*where* else. He was dying.

She felt tears trickle down her cheeks, didn't think he'd be able to speak—but he did, his voice the barest whisper. She leaned closer, her hair sticking to her wet face.

"Guess . . . this is it," he slurred out. "I'm—cold . . ."

"I'm sorry, I'm so sorry," she whispered, the tears coming harder now, the truth a lump in her throat. "I can't do anything for you—"

He had closed his eyes but now opened them again, a tiny flicker of life behind his shiny wet gaze. "Yes," he breathed, then coughed, sprayed her with tiny droplets of bloody mist.

"Don't . . . don't let them . . ." He coughed again, tried to turn his head but couldn't. "Don't let him . . . please, kill me . . ."

Somehow she'd known what he would ask, but his question was just as terrifying, as disturbing as she'd feared it would be. Her heart cried out in anguish, her mind reeling.

"No, I can't, don't make me—"

It was as if he hadn't heard her. "Then . . . kill Church . . . got to . . . kill him . . ."

He kept her gaze with his, the effort of speaking obviously an agony.

"Please . . . Sharon, please . . ."

The word became a litany, a soft, dying chant, over and over. She could see the rest of it in his eyes, the plea they held.

Don't let it be for nothing, Sharon. Don't let me die for nothing.

"Please . . . please . . ."

She leaned over him, kissed his forehead with trembling lips, her tears falling into his hair. She moved back, cradled his head and chin in her hands, her mind blank, her strength gathering.

Tony Crespi closed his eyes, his brow smooth now, unfettered.

"Rest now," she whispered, and with a single, swift movement, turned his head, the sickening crack of his spine loud in the silent corridor.

28

She just sat there for a moment, holding him, lacking the strength to even cry for him. He had been a good man, an honest man—and in the end, he'd had to beg for death, cradled in the arms of a woman he hardly even knew.

She keened, a high, wailing note that made her want to weep—and yet only a single tear escaped, the pain suddenly too great for mere sobs. Regrets for the friendship they might have had, sorrow for his painful death—she was exhausted, felt immersed in her misery.

"*. . . Sharon, please . . .*"

After a time she gently lay his head on the floor and stood, looking down at his still form. The lines of pain were gone, at least, his expression one of peace—

From somewhere beyond the open door, she heard the piteous scream of the wounded drone echo through the labyrinth, a sound as bereaved as her own, anguished and in pain. Another victim . . .

McGuinness straightened and turned, felt a huge, sudden unnameable thing well up inside of her, something like rage but *more*. This was a cold thing, an icy hand that gripped her heart and sent pulses of liquid nitrogen coursing through her veins. She wasn't overwhelmed by it; it simply engulfed her, swallowed her up. She *became* the thing, felt her sadness disappear as if it had never been.

McGuinness walked for the door, unhurried, her steps firm and deliberate.

She had a promise to keep.

Church studied the monitor closely, confused. The drone had run. His perfect killing machine had *run*, and he didn't know why, it was unprecedented, *unheard* of—

He saw McGuinness snap the dying man's neck and then mourn for him, her lament almost painful to watch—except that the sight was infuriating, the waste devastating; Crespi's brain would be a patternless mush by the time he could get to it. The drone should have killed them *both*; he could have been there in less than a minute to collect his specimens . . .

He tracked the drone on a smaller screen, saw it cowering at a dead end in one of the tunnels, its head dripping diluted acid on the alloyed floor, its muted shrieks pathetic from pain. Why had it fled? Drones were *driven* by pain, by everything, single-minded in their purpose. It simply wasn't *possible*—

And yet it had happened; there had to be a reason, some fluke, an anomaly, surely . . .

Yes, that was it. He nodded to himself, relieved. A freak occurrence, a *rarity*—the drone's instinctual behavior had been altered somehow by the damaging blow; perhaps it had destroyed the psychic center, rendering the creature blind—

"Church!"

Startled, he looked back to the main tracker, the camera on McGuinness. She stared straight at him, her fists clenched at her sides, her face cold and unblinking.

"Church, do you hear me?! I'm going to *kill* you, you bastard!"

He stared back at her, tried to find his confidence, the knowledge of the Truth, suddenly lost in a cool wave of—

Fear?

No. He wouldn't have it, *would not*.

Church stabbed at another button, raised the door to the first chamber. The two drones there moved quickly, past Crespi's dead body, their senses seeking out the live, moving prey.

He wanted her dead.

Now.

She jogged through the labyrinth, still that cold thing, choosing her path by instinct. She didn't know what had happened to her, and she didn't care; it was what she *was* now and she would achieve her goal by it—

A machine, a drone, I have become an instrument for something beyond what I know . . .

Yes. And it was unimportant; all that mattered was that she get to Church and do what must be done. Behind her, she heard the hisses and shrieks of at least two of the drones, their hard bodies clattering, reverberating through the dark, lonely halls.

Have to circle back, get to that pen, get to Church—

She had no doubts, no fear, except for a detached, almost clinical concern that she would be killed before she could finish—it was analyzed and discarded quickly, set aside as an improbability. Her hot, desperate terror from before was nothing but a hazy dream, as if it had happened to somebody else.

No decisive plan came to mind as she hurried along, no great revelations as to how she would make it. She wouldn't be able to outrun the aliens, probably couldn't hide as they went past—they'd *sense* her, or Church would simply shock her out of whatever cranny she could find.

She wondered coolly why he hadn't already killed her that way, fried her to death—but even as she thought it, she knew why. His ego wouldn't allow for it, wouldn't allow for such an anticlimactic ending. He wanted her to die screaming, struggling beneath the nightmare creatures . . .

He'd be disappointed. But, then, he'd be dead.

She only hoped that he'd be cocky enough to unseal that first door, his desire to watch her die in person overriding his caution. She thought it was probable—though if she was wrong . . .

If I'm wrong, I'll find another way.

The thought instantly quelled her vague concern; if there was a way, it would be done.

She reached another split in the labyrinth, veered right without even thinking about it. Behind, the sounds of the running drones came closer.

Church watched as McGuinness ran, seemingly choosing her path at random. The two slavering creatures stumbled along not far behind, slowed by their hunger, but they were still faster than she was; it wouldn't be long now . . .

He felt some of the lost confidence returning, settle back over him comfortably. Now that the end of the experiment was drawing near, he felt a momentary regret, that he had given in to his weakness earlier. If he'd held out, Crespi might not have been wasted . . .

McGuinness took another passage, once again without hesitation—and he saw where she was headed.

Church grinned, punched at the entry button for the kennel. Marvelous! She'd be joining him for a last hurrah, perhaps make up for having ruined Crespi's chemical analysis . . .

She paused suddenly, stood still in corridor D, her face not expressing the uncertainty she must be feeling. Her chest heaved, her hair slick with sweat. She was tiring quickly, was probably almost done running—

Church laughed brightly, hoping that she'd make it back to the open enclosure before his little pets caught up to her . . .

He wanted to see her pleading eyes when she begged him for a quick death.

*　　*　　*

McGuinness made another turn, running easily now having caught her second wind. She didn't question the instinctual drive that had taken her this far, didn't wonder how she *knew*; she just did, in no uncertain terms. She was headed back to Church.

Suddenly the instinct spoke, a single word.

Wait.

She stopped where she was, breathing heavily, her mind clear and open. Just the one word, and she obeyed, knew as surely as she knew her name that it wouldn't steer her wrong.

It had sounded a lot like Crespi.

The drones moved closer to her, their shadowy forms loping through the maze, tracking her fear—

They were almost to the opening to D corridor, seconds away from her unmoving form. Church gave up on seeing it live, leaned closer to the monitor—

The drones turned down the wrong passage.

Church half rose from his seat, shocked. "WHAT—"

They ran through the empty passage, hissing and screaming, headed *away* from her, headed—

The damaged drone, still crouching, bleeding, moaning in pain.

It had no psychic ability.

It was blind, afraid.

And they didn't recognize it as one of their own.

He watched, horrified, stunned, as they fell on the injured creature, their talons ripping into it, their jaws snapping. The drone shrieked, fought back in its terror, gripped one of its attackers by the harness and *twisted*, the harnessed creature falling, its screams of pain—

Of death.

It crumpled to the cold floor, twitching spasmodically.

The second attacker leapt forward, clawed at the killer's back, at the dorsal nerve center. The killer faltered, fell across the dead thing in front of it, too injured now to fight anymore.

And then there was one . . .

Church was numb, astonished. He'd never considered the *possibility*—

Movement again, a flicker at the corner of his vision. He looked back at the D monitor, suddenly *afraid* again, this *was not happening*!

McGuinness was coming.

She heard the voice again, accepted it.

—go—

She went.

Church slammed his hand against the electrical pulse, shocking the last drone out of its halted crouch.

It screamed, pivoted its head, searching—

—and found its mark. She was moving again and the other drones were dead; it ran back down the passage, frenzied in its hunt.

Church exhaled raggedly. He was in control again. And McGuinness was as good as dead.

* * *

McGuinness circled right, then ran straight ahead, the light growing brighter, almost blindingly so. A final turn—

She ran into the kennel, panting, just in time to see Church step to the railing, a smile on his despicable, ugly face.

She'd made it.

She started for him, walking across the floor of the large pen, could feel the ice inside that was more than anger, the snarl that formed across her features. There were no coherent thoughts, no words, nothing that could describe the depths of loathing and hatred that filled her at the sight of him, still so cold, unemotional in their pure intensity—

From the chamber behind her, an alien screamed, coming fast.

Church smiled down at her, tried not to look relieved when he heard the drone's cry, close now.

"McGuinness," he said easily. "I *am* surprised! You're going to give me some beautiful chemicals ..."

That look on her face. Why was she looking *like that?*

He reached for the handheld buzzer, grasped it tightly. "... and then I think I can arrange for you and Lennox to spend some quality time together."

She stalked across the pen, still snarling at him, her eyes cold.

Behind her, the drone.

Church smiled wider, relaxed. "Uh-oh, here comes your dance partner—"

Suddenly she leapt straight up, grabbed at one of his cameras, designed to defy a talon's grasp—

He punched the buzzer automatically, but he was too late. She was above the field of range, holding on to the alloyed camera with *one hand*, knees drawn to her chest, her knuckles white—

The drone shrieked in pain. Church released the switch quickly, breath suddenly tight.

No, no—

The alien recovered almost immediately, jumped for her before she could move—and knocked her down, hard. McGuinness hit the floor and spun around, dwarfed by the starving creature that reached out, drooling—

Church allowed a true smile; it was finished.

McGuinness screamed, but not in fear, not in the begging cries that he'd anticipated. A sound of pure, primal rage poured out of her, her teeth bared, her fists raised, her face kissing distance from the drone's snapping jaws—

The drone lowered its head, paused—

And then backed slowly away.

29

McGuinness looked away from the groveling creature, somehow not at all surprised that it had backed away. She was cold inside, cold and deadly; the drone understood.

She turned her killing gaze to Church.

"You're *dead*," she snarled, and jumped, grasped the slick camera again, and started to pull herself up.

His expression was a caricature of shock and disbelief; he seemed to forget the device in his hand, seemed to have forgotten *everything* in his blatant rejection of the truth.

"But there's no telepathine in your—" he began, then apparently realized what was about to happen.

"Fuck your telepathine, you're *dead*," she said again, liking the feel of the words in her mouth.

He jabbed at the buzzer again and again, frantic.

The creature below screamed horribly, but McGuinness was not to be turned, distracted.

"I want you *dead*—"

Still sounded right, sounded like truth; she could not hate him enough.

For David.

For Crespi.

For all she had lost, *dead*. For the lives that had been shaded and blasphemed by this creature, *dead*. For his egomaniacal pomposity, his glittering, cursed gaze, his wretched smile . . .

Your blood for them; your life *for them.*

The climb was effortless, easier than blinking, and still she wasn't surprised. Camera to the lowest rail, a grunt of minor exertion as she pulled herself up, gripped the top rail—and climbed over it, seething with the icy, crystal hatred, the promise she intended to keep.

Church took one fumbling step backward, still not believing, she saw it on his stupid face, the frightened wonder in his eyes. He was an abomination, an atrocity; he was an insult to life.

One step forward and she had him.

His strength was nothing; if he tried to defend himself, she didn't know, couldn't tell. She snatched at his hair, at the back of his lab coat, and flung him forward to the rail, smashed his idiot face into the smooth, hard metal.

He still seemed surprised as his nose shattered, a single, clueless bark of dismay emerging muffled and wet. Blood splashed down into the kennel, spattered across his pristine coat, the pattern intricate, infinitely beautiful to her cold eyes.

He struggled as she pressed harder, grinding the

cartilage to the rail, heard the wet *crunch* sound and found it to be music.

From far away, she heard voices, pounding. Someone was trying to get in, alerted by the screams of the drone . . .

Where the fuck were you an hour ago? she thought vaguely, then yanked his head back and drove it forward again. One of his cheekbones gave with a slippery *snap*, an epiphany.

Gunfire outside. They were coming.

She spun him around, twisted him so that he was facing her, saw the fear in his eyes and felt *good*, felt that he was finally starting to understand—

Below them, the drone screamed, awake. Hungry.

She shot a glance downward, the capering creature eager and frantic at the taste of blood, its tortured shrieks alive with frustration and hunger. The alien had been tormented throughout Church's sick crucible, taken from its home, starved, shocked, teased with the promise of escape and the scents of fresh meat. Its black exoskeleton was dull, matte, a bird with rotting feathers; it was dying, its siblings already dead, and all for Paul Church's great Truth . . .

McGuinness grinned, felt no humor in the expression. Even Church would have to appreciate the irony.

She clasped her hands together, swung back—

"Freeze!"

—glanced behind her, saw the guards rushing in, rifles drawn—

—and brought her giant fist forward, hitting Church in the chest, knocking him backward over the rail. He screamed, clutched vainly at the air.

"I said *freeeeeze*—"

McGuinness stepped to the railing, looked over,

saw the drone scamper for Church, reach for him with spindly claws, saw the dread shrivel him, shrink him—

Then the guards were there, shouting, rifles pointed down into the kennel.

"Doctor Church! Get away from it! I can't get a clean shot!"

The drone *had* him, clutched his small head in its hands, jaws dripping—

McGuinness pushed the shouting guard, turned to the other, ready to kill them if necessary—

The last thing she saw was a rifle butt coming at her.

The sound of shots followed her down into the darkness.

30

How are you feeling, Doctor?"

Church looked up from his reading, saw Admiral Thaves's bulk filling the doorway. He sighed inwardly but smiled at Thaves, lay his remote on the nightstand.

"Better, Admiral. Actually, I'm quite well enough to get back to work—"

Thaves shook his head. "Forget it. The meds say another week."

The admiral looked around the bare sickbay room as if he'd never seen it before, hadn't visited every couple of days for the last three weeks. The room was small but comfortable, the walls a pale green, muted; a place of rest. When he spoke again, his voice was soft, almost gentle.

"Everything okay?"

Church folded his hands, stared down at them absently. It was a question that had plagued him for many days now. "I ... I keep thinking of McGuinness."

That much is true ...

Thaves scowled, transforming his face from merely ugly to ugly and mean, a fleeting glimpse of a much younger Thaves, a man of no small means, a man to reckon with—a stern flash of how he had made his stars, of war days long past.

Only an instant, then gone. "Hell, *you* saw the recordings! She was a cold-blooded murderer, killed Crespi with her bare hands—and might've killed you, 'cept for the guards."

Thaves smiled, his old self again. He was probably attempting a look of reassurance, though it came as an apology, as embarrassment. "The Marines picked her up yesterday; don't worry about her coming back, either."

Church sighed, careful not to reveal the rest of it; Thaves could never know, *wouldn't* know, would stay oblivious to the human emotions that they surely shared in this matter. Church reached up absently to finger the small bandage across his nose. "It's not that. Some of the things she said ... about *me*. I suppose it has me thinking whether my work here is— wrong."

Thaves frowned, walked to the bed, and rested his weight against the frame. His face turned serious, his gaze firm and unwavering.

"She was insane, Paul. Your work—your research has saved countless lives, you need to remember that.

Why, if it weren't for your viral tent, my own *daughter* wouldn't be alive today—"

Church nodded humbly; Thaves had great affection for his youngest, an affection that had allowed Church to write his own rules on board the station. Thaves signed releases, ordered transports to bring new people to the station, and turned a blind eye to the fact that many of those people he had never met—and never would.

Church wondered absently how Thaves would react if he knew what was really going on—and he commended himself once again for having the presence of mind to lock up his private lab before that last miserable experiment.

The admiral was still speaking. "—so don't worry over anything that crazy bitch accused you of, no one believed a word. You're a good man, Paul."

Church actually considered the statement for a moment, the implications of his own humanity. In any sense, "good" was not what came to mind.

"Think where it got Crespi," Church said quietly.

The admiral dropped his serious pep-talk look for the much rarer false sympathy one, feeling blindly for some connection to an emotional realm; Church was not the only being that had to search, to fake. He never had been.

"I'm—sorry about Crespi. You two really hit it off, I guess."

Church looked down, counted to three slowly. On the last count, Thaves slapped the edge of the mattress and stood, signaling the end of his visit.

"Well, I guess you could use some rest! I'll stop by tomorrow, see how you're doing."

Church smiled up at him gratefully. "That would be

nice, Admiral—and thanks for coming. It means a lot
to me."

"Nothing of it," he blustered, and Church could see
the pleasure in his rough face before he turned and
walked out.

It was ... *appealing* to affect someone that way, to
bring a measure of contentment to his fellow man,
even an overblown and pathetic individual like
Thaves; indeed, the lowest of creatures deserved
some happiness, he had come to believe. Thaves was
a throwaway character in his own drama, but he
could still *feel*. Strange, how things changed ...

Church stared blankly at the wall for a moment,
thinking about McGuinness. She was gone, finally. He
was almost embarrassed by the cool relief that had
flooded through him at the admiral's confirmation; almost, but not quite. He tried not to make lying to himself a practice, and the core truth was that she had
scared him, and scared him badly.

She'd been like a drone when she'd come after
him, mindless except for the sole motive of slaughter,
her movements as physically able and as driven with
purpose; a drone of his own making, but in a way he'd
never expected.

Church shuddered involuntarily and reached for
the remote. He needed to clear his head of her, fill his
thoughts with something besides the remembrance of
his fear ...

He clicked a button, activated the wheelchair at the
foot of his bed. He *had* managed to get some work
done, unofficially of course. He'd head to the lab,
check on the progress of a few things, crowd the
woman out with comforting routine.

He slid into the chair, steeling himself for pain, but

there was hardly any now; the worst had been his face, the cheekbone, but the leg fracture from the fall had been an agony unto itself.

The drone, reaching, the blood in his eyes turning it red and impossibly more *manic, the sudden meeting of fates, the* terror—*and the sharp pain as his leg gave way, the acid burns that quilted his human flesh as the bullets found their mark*—

It was late, the bay empty, though no one would have stopped him anyway; the meds were fine for stern warnings, but their follow-through was somewhat lacking—particularly for him. He had known for some time that the station was truly under *his* command, but had only come to appreciate it in the last few weeks.

He rode toward the supply storage area, the wheels rolling noiselessly against the smooth floor. He had to strain to reach the door control, but again, no real pain; he'd be out sooner than a week, surely.

The entry slid open, revealed the seldom-used passage that he'd come to know intimately in the past days. It was quite something, the *Innominata;* the entire station was one great labyrinth, silent corridors connecting everything to everything else, every door opening beneath his touch to disclose yet another path . . .

Surprises. There had been too many lately, too many revelations that were frightening in their quiet subtlety. When he'd told his story to Crespi and McGuinness, he'd been unable to focus on that *feeling*, the influence it had had on him—and still, he didn't know. What he *did* know was that it would not leave him now, the memories, the vision of his mother's dying face . . .

He could no longer dismiss his past.

The chair slid down the dim hall, in and out of the shadows, veering first to the right and then again, then left and down a sloping decline.

He felt fine, he supposed, should feel better than fine now that McGuinness was gone; but ever since the attack, he'd somehow mislaid his sense of humor. Everything seemed—*tainted* now, as if the colors around him had all muted a shade, nothing as bright as it used to be.

You're just bedsore, Doctor. You'll see—once you're on your feet again, all will be well . . .

He *hoped* so, wanted it to be true—but felt certain just the same that he would never again be as confident as before. He'd made mistakes, had let things escape his control . . . and he had inspired a practical stranger to a depth of hatred beyond any he'd ever known . . .

Things *were* different. The humanity that he'd shunted aside for so long had come back, whispering to him, coaxing him. First had been fear, but now others, simple, pleasant feelings that were *not* the wry amusement he had known, a "soul searching" that gave him pause at every turn. The essence of the Truth had been clouded by these things, would perhaps be lost if he did not take care—

And that would be so tragic? So debilitating?

There was no answer to that, not now.

Sighing, he reached for the code slate as the chair stopped, reversed, pulled up beside the plug for the round, gleaming hatch in front of him. He inserted it, punched a button, waited.

The door opened and the chair moved forward,

slowly now, rested midway across the floor of his small, private lab.

He looked at the large holding tank that dominated the room, noted the minute changes of the form inside. He smiled a little; things were progressing quite well, actually. Infinitely better than his last attempt.

The once human form had grown a semisynthetic plate system, dark in color, ridges of bone mutating, transforming, *becoming*. Spines extended from the shoulders, and he could see where something like a dorsal fin had appeared, perhaps the aquatic influence—

He focused on the face, and his smile faded. As always, he could think of nothing to say, no one thing that would explain how he felt. And as always, he tried anyway.

"I . . . I hope you know, Tony. None of this is personal."

The dark, unconscious form of Anthony Crespi made no reply.

But then, none was expected.

Epilogue

McGuinness slept the deep sleep, her chamber by itself inside a locked cell as the transport ship hurtled toward Earth.

She dreamed of promises made and promises broken. She dreamed of a man she had once loved, and another man she might have loved, given enough time. And finally, she dreamed of a being that wasn't human at all, with claws and teeth and long white hair. A thing she had tried to kill but had not been strong enough to succeed.

In her dreams, she went back.

And this time, she was stronger.

ABOUT THE AUTHOR

S. D. (STEPHANI DANELLE) PERRY has written two other graphic novel adaptations in the *Aliens* series—*Aliens: The Female War* and *Aliens vs. Predator: Prey*—both with her father, Steve Perry. She also adapted the script *Timecop* for Dark Horse, and has sold two short stories, one to *Pulphouse Hardcover #11* and one to the first *Magic: The Gathering* anthology.

S. D. Perry currently lives in Portland, Oregon, with her artist fiancé and their corgi, H. P. Lovecraft, and divides her time between wedding plans and work on her own independent horror novels.

The adventures continue in

ALIENS™ *vs.* PREDATOR™

ONE IS A RACE OF RUTHLESS and intractable killers, owing their superiority to pure genetics. The other uses the trappings of high technology to render themselves the perfect warriors. Now, the classic conflict of heredity vs. environment, nature vs. nurture, is played out in a larger—and bloodier—arena: the universe.

ALIENS VS. PREDATOR: PREY _____56555-9
by Steve Perry and Stephani Perry $4.99/$6.50 in Canada
ALIENS VS. PREDATOR: HUNTER'S PLANET _____56556-7
by David Bischoff $4.99/$6.50 in Canada

And don't forget

PREDATOR™

THE ULTIMATE HUNTERS HAVE landed. Drawn by heat and the thrill of the chase, these alien warriors have one goal in mind: to locate the ultimate prey. The wilier, the smarter, the more formidable the foe, the more it increases their delight. For all is sport to them, and we are their favorite game.

PREDATOR: CONCRETE JUNGLE _____56557-5
by Nathan Archer $4.99/$6.50 in Canada